Readers love
PARKER WILLIAMS

Before You Break

"With finesse and care, the writing team of Wells and Williams leads us into a world where men care for each other and dare to be vulnerable while still maintaining their need to be masters of their own destinies."

—The Novel Approach

"Whether you have read Collars and Cuffs or not, this is a wonderful entry book to an enchanting new series."

—Happy Ever After, *USA Today*

Endings and Beginnings

"*Endings and Beginnings* has everything a great series finale should, including laughs, tears, new milestones, and a guarantee of future happiness for everyone involved."

—Sinfully: Gay Romance Book Reviews

"Overall, this is an amazing, emotional ending to a brilliant series. The Collars and Cuffs Series will always be one of my all time favorites."

—Rainbow Gold Reviews

By PARKER WILLIAMS

Runner

With K.C. Wells
Before You Break

COLLARS AND CUFFS
An Unlocked Heart
Trusting Thomas
Someone to Keep Me
A Dance with Domination
Damian's Discipline
Make Me Soar
Dom of Ages
Endings and Beginnings

Published by DREAMSPINNER PRESS
www.dreamspinnerpress.com

RUNNER

PARKER WILLIAMS

Published by

DREAMSPINNER PRESS

5032 Capital Circle SW, Suite 2, PMB# 279, Tallahassee, FL 32305-7886 USA
www.dreamspinnerpress.com

Runner
© 2017 Parker Williams.

Cover Art
© 2017 Reese Dante.
http://www.reesedante.com
Cover content is for illustrative purposes only and any person depicted on the cover is a model.

ISBN: 978-1-63533-810-2
Digital ISBN: 978-1-63533-811-9
Library of Congress Control Number: 2017903377
Published July 2017
v. 1.0

Printed in the United States of America

This paper meets the requirements of
ANSI/NISO Z39.48-1992 (Permanence of Paper).

To everyone who told me I could do it, this book is for you.

ACKNOWLEDGMENTS

TO BECKY Condit, Mary Phillips Wallace, Hannah Walker, LM Somerton, K.C. Wells, Cate Ashwood, Tracy C. Muth, and others who wanted to hold Matt.

And a special thank you to Tricia Kristufek and everyone at Dreamspinner Press for giving me this opportunity!

CHAPTER ONE

THERE WERE 376 steps from one end of my property to the other. Not that I'd walked them, mind you, but I counted them as the man who jogged past every day, rain or shine, made his way down the road. I'd begun to accept his presence in my world, but it didn't start out that way. At first I found him to be a terrifying intrusion. I hated people anywhere near my house. I'd moved to the outskirts of my hometown of Fall Harbor, Maine, for just that reason. After what happened, I needed to be alone. And now this guy seemed intent on destroying my peace.

My place wasn't on the beaten path. Hell, if truth be told, you had to actively come out this way to find it, because it took almost thirty minutes by car to reach the town square twenty miles away. I valued my privacy, and I paid a great deal to ensure I kept it.

Then he came along.

The first several days after I spotted him, I cowered in my home, because seeing him so close disturbed me. It had been better than a month since the last time I'd seen someone on my road, which really went nowhere. After you made the turn down the way, it became a dead end that forced you to turn around and come back the same path. Which meant I saw him twice a day. And twice a day I went into a near meltdown.

Because of him, gone were the days I saw no one, interacted with not a single soul. I had it arranged so my lawyer took care of any bills, I grew most of my own food, and what I couldn't grow was delivered to the edge of my lot, where, after much inspection, it could be brought into the house, sorted, and put away in its proper place. All that changed the day he huffed past my house and turned my world upside down.

He couldn't be more than thirty, with brown hair that came down to his collar and slapped him in the face when it dripped with sweat as he ran. His toned body seemed to be acres of golden skin, dusted with a light coating of soft brown fur. Yes, I looked. In fact, I studied him in detail, this threat to my sanity.

It seemed as though his existence altered the feng shui of the place. Not that I believed in that, of course. But everything had to be just so, and any deviation left me out of sorts. I knew the deer that crossed my land every day, stopping to nibble on the tender shoots in the spring, then huddled against the cold in the deepest of winter. There had been a family of lark sparrows nesting in one of my trees every year since I'd gotten here, and I woke to their song in the morning. The black and bright yellow sunflowers I planted every eighteen inches in front of the house bloomed together, a product of water and sunshine. It all had to be just so.

Then he came along.

I thought, after the first day, he'd disappear. It would have made me happy, because huddling beneath my window angered me. I had no idea how or why he came here, because this road wasn't made for running. With the steep hills and sharp curves, it could actually be pretty treacherous.

The first time I saw him, it took me nearly eight hours to calm myself. I had to go through and touch everything to ensure it was still in place, because my hands shook until I did. Then he came back the next day, and the cycle repeated itself.

I tried calling the sheriff, but he laughed and assured me no law existed about people running on the road. When I protested, he got snippy.

"Did he come onto your property?" he asked, and I could hear the annoyance in his clipped cadence.

"Well, no, but—"

"Then I'm sorry, Matt. I can't do anything about it. He's free to run wherever he sees fit."

"Can't you at least suggest he find somewhere else?" I pleaded.

When his voice took on the pitying tone I knew so well, I wanted to hang up. "You know, it would do you good to have some company out there," he told me. "Maybe you should try to talk to the man. Invite him in for some of that weird tea you brew up."

"Mom could tell you to do it," I countered.

Yeah, the sheriff, Clayton Bailey Bowers, was, by two years, my younger brother.

"Pretty sure that Mom would agree with me," he drawled. "She doesn't like you living out in the woods like that anyway. Why can't you come back to town and live like…."

He paused a breath too long.

"Like a normal person?" I demanded. "That's what you were going to say, right?"

Clay let loose with a long, aggrieved sigh. "It's been thirteen years, Matt. You won't come to see Mom or me. You won't allow us to come and visit you. Hell, even your friends have stopped asking after you."

Friends. I suppose that's what they thought they were, but I never had that connection with them. "Acquaintances" I'd have to agree to, but not much beyond that. Ever since what's referred to by most people as "the incident," I've had the need to be alone, to stay as far away from people as I can. The incident shattered my world, and now I desperately needed to make sure I held it together. It's why familiarity had become so important to me.

I was a high school student at the time. We'd celebrated my sixteenth birthday three weeks before that, and Mom had gotten me a beater car, a lemon-yellow Toyota with nearly seventy thousand miles on it. The car was well traveled, and every time I drove her, I imagined we were taking part in history. I loved that car, probably more than my brother at the time. If I'd had to choose between him and the car… well, it was a good thing the situation never came up.

We'd been having some weird weather that spring. A lot of rain, sometimes even mixed with snow. Then the next day, the temperatures would soar into the eighties. One of the teachers, Mr. Jackson, told me his car had died in the parking lot, and he wondered if I could give him a ride home. I never liked the man. He gave off this creepy vibe, and a lot of people commented on it. But like an idiot, I said sure. His smile and cheery thanks made my stomach queasy.

He gave me directions, and I found myself in a field pretty far from town. Everything in me screamed to turn around and go back, but I swallowed down my fear.

"You live out here? It's kind of far from school."

He put an arm around me and pulled me close. Oh my God, the hair on the back of my neck stood up, and I tried to push away from him, but he held fast, bringing his mouth to mine. In a panic, I laid on the horn. He jerked back, his pupils blown. He gave me some sort of sick grin and leaned forward again. I tried to hit him as I screamed for him to get away from me.

"You knew why we were coming out here," Mr. Jackson said, grabbing a handful of my hair. And the sick thing was he seemed genuinely certain I'd come out here for that reason.

"No, I didn't!" I shouted as I continued to struggle with someone twice my age, who stood at least six inches more than my five foot eight inches and outweighed me by a good forty pounds. "You asked for a ride home, and that's what I thought you wanted. I don't want this with you."

I struggled to get away, but his grip tightened. I didn't give a damn if he yanked out every hair on my head; I did not want his hands on me. Lashing out, I hit him in the face. He snarled and grabbed me with his other hand. He had me now, both hands with a death grip on my head. He tried to force me down toward his crotch. The sweaty, musty smell made my stomach roil and my head swim. He let go with one hand and fumbled with his belt, his breath coming in ragged gasps.

"Please don't do this," I begged. "I won't tell anyone."

Then it struck me. What would he do to me after? He had to know I'd tell my mother or someone. Did he think they wouldn't believe me? Would he hurt me—or worse—after he got what he wanted? I started to cry.

"Shh. It's okay," Mr. Jackson murmured. "I'll take care of you."

He peeled back his underwear and his cock popped out. The smell became overpowering and I... threw up. All over his lap with the vegetable pizza they'd served for lunch. That, added to the odor of his crotch, had me heaving everywhere. He pushed me away, then hit me, hard, in the face. It dazed me, and I thought he'd overpower me. Instead he got out, dragged me from the car, and pushed me to the dirt. He kicked me in the ribs once or twice, then got in my little lemon and drove away.

I shivered, and not from the cold. His hands on me, his mouth touching mine. They'd chilled me to my depths. I crawled to the nearest tree and sat against it, the rough bark digging into my arms, and cried.

FOUR HOURS later, the sheriff at the time, Roy Campbell, and my mom found me. She hurried from the squad car and threw her arms around me, and I sank into the embrace, sobbing how sorry I was.

"Shh. You didn't do anything wrong," she assured me.

But I did. I let him into my car—my life—even though I didn't feel right about it. Everything that happened was because of me.

The sheriff stood behind her, not meeting my gaze. His body language told me he found the whole thing uncomfortable. I wasn't really surprised. He'd never been the most tolerant of people who weren't like him. When Mom turned her glare on him and demanded that he get off his goddamn ass and do something, he snapped into action. He started by asking me if I was okay—had he hurt me? I barked a laugh, because my face hadn't gotten swollen all by itself. When he knelt down and reached toward me, I jerked away.

"No, don't touch me!" I screamed.

He pulled his hand back as if he'd been zapped. Mom bundled me up and got me into the cruiser, then sat beside me, pulling me into her embrace. She stroked my hair, murmuring to me that it would be okay, but even back then I knew the truth. Nothing would ever be the same again.

They took me to the hospital, where I was given some painkillers and told I needed plenty of rest. They released me the next morning when Mom came to get me. She hurried me to the car and got in beside me. She didn't say anything on the drive home, and I was grateful for that. My mind was already jumbled with replaying the incident from every angle to see what I should have done differently. Unfortunately nothing seemed to change, no matter how many times I went through it. I'd done something to make him think I was willing. I just didn't know what.

That night, Mom told me she'd seen Mr. Jackson flying through town in the car she'd given me, brakes squealing as he turned the corner. She knew something had to be wrong. She went to the sheriff and convinced him to check into it. When they caught Mr. Jackson at his home, he first told them I'd loaned him my car because his wasn't working. Mom said that was a lie. She knew I'd sooner give up Clay than I would my car. The sheriff arrested Mr. Jackson and took him to the tiny office he worked out of. Crime in our town wasn't unknown, but mostly it consisted of bored kids being somewhere they shouldn't. When Mr. Jackson told them where he'd left me, he tried to say it had been consensual, that I'd come on to him. My mom freaked out over that, because she knew better. She and Clay knew I was gay, but she also knew I would never do anything with a grown-up, and certainly not in our small town. Mr. Jackson finally confessed, was charged with attempted rape, and went to trial. Fortunately, since he admitted his guilt, our lawyer said I wouldn't have to testify.

It never changed anything for me, though. My life had started a downhill slide I thought I'd never get out of.

"We got your car back," Mom told me later.

My beloved car. The most precious thing in my life. Now it was tainted. I didn't think I could bear to see it again. "Sell it," I said.

"But you love that car."

"I don't want it anymore."

"You'll feel better one day. You'll see." Her voice was filled with a hope I didn't feel.

I stayed home from school for the next two weeks, talking to no one. Mom tried to coax me out of my room with my favorite dinner, but I said I wasn't hungry. Eventually she put a plate outside the door and left me in peace, which I appreciated. My whole world had begun to crumble around me. Everywhere I looked, I saw reminders of the kid I'd been. The stupid person who believed that helping people could never be a bad thing. I began to straighten up my room to give me something to do. I found that as I made order from the chaos around me, my mind calmed and I could breathe again. Every trophy, every kitschy little thing I'd bought over the years, all my pictures… they were the bits and pieces that made up my life. If I hoped to find my center, they had to be perfect. I sorted them, first by color, then by year, and finally by size. Next came the books on my bookshelf. Genre first, then author name. I made lists of where everything was so I could always find it with ease.

By the time I stepped out of my bedroom, I'd calmed. But then I noticed the mess of the house and felt the urge to fix it. It was part of what I considered to be mine, and I didn't like to see it messy. Mom had gone to work, Clay to school, so there was no one else in the house. I set to cleaning. I dusted, then washed down the walls and floors before I tackled the rest of the house. By the time everyone got home, I'd made a sizable dent, but so much more remained to be done.

"Clay? Go on up to your room, okay?" Mom asked.

"Sure, but can he come and do mine next?" Clay asked, his voice breaking when he laughed.

"Get upstairs," Mom snapped.

Clay trudged up the stairs, mumbling under his breath the whole way.

"Honey, come and sit down."

"I can't," I protested. I had hours of work ahead of me to get the place... right.

"Matt," she coaxed.

I put the sponge into the bucket, then squeezed it out and lined it up beside the pail. I turned to her and saw the worry in her guarded expression.

"What are you doing?"

I blew out a breath. "Just cleaning."

"Honey, you're sixteen. Boys don't clean when they're that age. Hell, your father didn't clean when he was in his thirties."

I wanted to laugh, but my gaze kept straying to the bucket. I inched a little closer to it, until Mom reached out and grabbed my wrist. I flinched and pulled away, then saw how hurt she looked. "I'm sorry," I whispered.

"No, I'm sorry. Matt, do you think... maybe we should see about getting you to talk to someone?"

After a few moments, I understood what she meant. "A shrink."

"A psychologist, yes. What he did to you wasn't right, and maybe you need someone who will help you understand it wasn't your fault."

Agitation welled within me, and I started stalking around the room, throwing my hands up as we talked. "But it was," I protested. "I mean, he thought I wanted it. He said so. So maybe deep down I did, and he noticed."

"Stop that!" Mom screamed, her face a mask of pain. "Just...." Her voice and expression softened. "Please, stop."

She tried to make me go to school, but when I got there, all I could see was the disarray. Nothing in the place it belonged, everything dirty. The kids were the worst, with their weird hair and their grungy clothes. Who could live like that? It struck me at that moment. He'd grabbed my hair, held me by it. Any one of these people I went to school with could do the same. Anyone could use my hair against me. The thought stayed with me throughout the day, as I ran my fingers through my blond locks. When I got home that night, I went to the bathroom to shower. After, I pulled out one of the safety razors Mom had bought me to shave with, and I cut off all my hair. It took several tries, and a lot of razors, but eventually my head was smooth.

When Mom saw me, she burst into tears. Clay found the whole thing hilarious.

Life changed for me after that. I stopped going to school, and eventually Mom quit begging me to go. I started to spend more and more time in my room, where order reigned. Mr. Jackson's lawyer got a plea bargain for him. He agreed to not fight the charges, for which we were grateful. It turned out that Mr. Jackson had received several reprimands from the school district but had never been formally disciplined. Our attorney went to court, saying they were culpable in the situation. Knowing they didn't have a leg to stand on, they paid the sum of three million dollars, which would be deposited in an account for me to collect when I turned eighteen. So Mr. Jackson went to prison for three years, and I started my lifelong sentence.

MOM WORRIED as my attitude swirled into depression. She made an appointment for me with a doctor, then dragged me to his office. At first I resisted, because the outside world was in such a sorry state.

I could see so many places where it could be better. When we got to the doctor's office, she introduced me to Dr. Robert Treadway. When he ushered me inside, a sense of peace prevailed.

I liked it there. For the most part, he had everything neat and organized, even if I saw a few places that could be better. When he saw me reaching to straighten something, he smiled and indulged me, allowing me to rearrange things to make more sense. Every week for the next three months, he'd let me come in and put things back the way I'd had them. I got comfortable in his office, as it seemed like an extension of me.

Our conversations were kept light. How was I feeling? How were things at home? Just surface stuff that I knew he was using to try to get into my head. Finally he got down to the big question.

"Do you want to talk about what happened with your teacher?" the doctor—"call me Rob"—asked.

"Not really, no."

I didn't want to even think about the man, but he lived in a corner of my mind and wouldn't go away. And to talk about it with the doctor? That would simply be reliving the whole mess again. Definitely not something I wanted to do.

"You know, it's not going to get better if we don't work on it together."

And wasn't that the crux of the situation? It wouldn't get better if we didn't talk about it, but talking about it would make me feel worse than I did because the memories would overwhelm me. I straightened the items on his desk, moving the penholder with a beautiful pair of gold Cross pens to the far corner of his desk.

"Why did you put it there?" he asked. "Last week you had it on the left side."

And I had. My hands started shaking when I reached for it again, but it looked right, even if my mind told me it wasn't.

"Matthew?"

No one called me that unless I'd done something to piss them off, but Rob said it in a nonthreatening kind of way, and I found it soothing.

"I don't know," I answered honestly. "It seemed like it should be there."

"That's a good enough answer. Sometimes when something feels more right in one place, it's okay to move it. Nothing needs to stay as it is forever."

But it did. Or at least it should. There could only be order if nothing moved after I put it in the proper place. But I hadn't lied; it did seem like it belonged more where I put it than on the other side of the desk. I'd noticed Rob was right-handed, and it seemed foolish to have it where he needed to stretch all the way across the desk to reach it.

He started again. "So. Your teacher. He changed his story quite often. Why do you think he said the first time you'd gone willingly?"

My gaze darted around the room, the feel of him being in the enclosed space with me nearly overwhelming. I could smell the stale sweat, hear him panting, feel his grip on my hair. My breath began to quicken and my body shook. In my mind I could hear his voice telling me that this was what I'd come for.

"It wasn't!" I shouted, pushing up out of the chair. "I didn't go there to have sex with him. I thought… I thought I was helping him out because his car didn't work. He lied to me, and I won't trust him again. I won't be stupid enough to trust anyone ever again." I turned to run for the door, but Rob's voice cut through the haze.

"Matthew, please sit down."

Sit down? Screw that. I wanted to run and never stop. Get away from the voice, from the memories that assailed me every night. Away from the nightmares that were my constant companions until I turned eighteen, gained the money that had been put aside for me, and bought my property, built a house, and removed myself from society.

Familiarity brought me peace, even if it took my mother and brother away from me.

A small price to pay, though, I told myself. Every night when I lay there, unable to sleep.

CHAPTER TWO

"ONE HUNDRED and sixteen, one hundred and seventeen, one hundred and eighteen...."

He kept an even pace, and I counted every footfall. His lean body moved with a fluid grace I might have been more than a little jealous of. When he turned in the direction of my house, he must have seen me watching him through the window, because he gave a little wave, then chugged on. I sputtered as my heart pounded and my mouth went dry. I closed the curtain, which made me lose my count and caused me to grow frustrated with the change in our... relationship. It had taken me six months to accept him near my property, and now he'd gone and messed up everything. Tomorrow I'd go back to fretting over seeing him, because now I had to wonder if he'd expect me to wave if I saw him, or worse, would want to stop and talk.

Despite repeated calls to Clay, he still refused to ask the man not to jog by my house. I pulled my phone out, sat down in the chair I had reupholstered, and dialed his number again.

"What is it this time, Matt?" Clay answered, his tone weary and unhappy.

"Please, Clay," I begged. "You've got to stop him."

He sighed. "Has something changed? Is he coming onto your property? Has he threatened you in any way?"

The temptation to say yes zipped through me, but he hadn't, and I couldn't lie.

"No," I replied, running my finger along the arm of the chair.

"What's wrong with him jogging down the road, Matt? I need something to go on before I can ask him to stop. Going up to him and saying, 'Do you mind not making my recluse of a brother uncomfortable?' won't really do much."

11

"Why do you have to be such an asshole?" I barked. "You know I don't like people near me, so why can't you just ask him nicely, as my brother if you won't do it as the sheriff, to find somewhere else to run?"

"Because...." He sighed again. It was something I heard pretty much every time I talked with him. "You know I love you, but I think you need to go back to see your doctor. You're not getting better."

It wasn't true. As long as people left me alone, I was fine. It was when they disrupted my life that things went wrong.

"I'm going to talk to Mom," he told me, his voice barely a whisper. "If you won't see someone on your own, then we'll have to see if Judge Hamlin can get you into a program."

Which was more shocking? That my brother and mother were conspiring against me, or that I knew if they went to see Hank "Happy" Hamlin, I'd be committed for sure. The man had never liked me when he'd been my teacher, so this little bit of retribution would probably send him over the moon.

"I'm not coming back to town," I insisted.

Clay made a humming noise, then said, "Okay, I'll tell you what. You prove to me that you're okay, and not only will I apologize to you, I won't ever bring it up again."

There had to be a trick somewhere, but I couldn't see it. "How do I prove it?"

He stayed quiet for a moment, and then I heard him chuckle. "Talk to the jogger."

"No!"

"It's that or you come home and see your therapist again. You know he wanted you to stay in your sessions. He thought you were making progress."

Only a shrink would say that night terrors and waking up in a cold sweat could be considered progress. Clay had me trapped, and the bastard knew it. There was no way I'd be able to get out of this. "Fine. I'll talk to the jogger."

"Oh no, bro," he said, his tone triumphant. "This isn't going to be you saying hello and that's it. It's not quite as simple as that. I need proof that you've done the deed."

"I'll save you a condom," I snarked.

"A world of ew. No, I'm going to make this very easy on you. All you have to do is tell me his name."

"That's it? Are you sure you don't want blood type, a DNA sample, or maybe his firstborn?"

"It's a small town. I'm sure I know everyone. You talk to him, tell me his name, and maybe I'll see what I can do to convince him that another route might be better for everyone concerned."

I tried to figure out a way to get him to change his mind, but knowing Clay, it wasn't about to happen. He'd always been stubborn, and it got him in plenty of hot water when we were kids. My heart thudded hard at the thought of having to talk to the man who'd been running past my property every day for the last six months, who now had acknowledged me.

"Please, Clay," I whispered, my voice cracking. "Don't make me do this."

"I'm sorry, Matt. I'm not doing this to hurt you. I want to know you're okay, and this is the only way I know how."

"But I can't," I whined. He had no idea how hard his request… shit, his demand would be. Even thinking about it had my hands shaking. Beyond my monthly calls to order my supplies, I hadn't talked to anyone except my brother—and that was only by phone— for several years. I hadn't even spoken to my mother, but that was for different reasons. Still, being out here was a balm to my soul. I likened it to an adventure, sort of like *My Side of the Mountain*, except without the hawk and I didn't live in a tree.

"Then you'll have to come home and talk to Robert. Those are your options, bro."

Now I knew what they meant by being stuck between a rock and a hard place. I held the phone between my shoulder and ear and wiped my damp palms over my pant legs. He'd left me no viable option, and the bastard knew it.

"Still there?" he asked.

I grabbed my phone again, then snapped, "Yes!" I took a deep breath. I couldn't have him changing his mind and simply going to the judge. Even though I hated the options given to me, at least they were there. I glanced around my house, looking at the sparse belongings I had. The centerpiece of my home was my bookcase, standing in the center of the wall, surrounded by smaller tables that held my trinkets and baubles. This wasn't about my fixation on order in my life, at least not entirely. I'd built a home here, and I had no desire to give it up.

"Okay," I told him. "I'll talk to him."

"Fine. You've got a week."

"What?" I spluttered. "You didn't say anything about a time limit."

Clay chuckled. "One of my favorite memories growing up is when you convinced me that skunk was the neighbor's new cat and told me to go pet it. Mom got so pissed when I came home, reeking of skunk spray, and you howled with laughter, even when she made you give me a tomato juice bath."

"Why are you telling me this?" I demanded, more than a little frustrated with Clay.

"Because I'm not that stupid anymore. I know if I don't make you do this within a certain time frame, you're going to hedge until I forget. That won't be happening either," he promised.

I sighed, leaning in the chair, resting my head along the back of it. "Fine. I'll do it within the week."

"The next time you call me, I want to know his name. No stalling for time, no prevarication, nothing. The only excuse you'll have is if he stops running by your house."

"How do you know I won't just say that?"

"Because it bothers you that he's doing it, and you won't be able to let it go. It will gnaw at you until you call me to complain again, and then we'll both know you lied."

I slumped into my chair and groaned. Growing up, especially after the incident, Clay had been both savior and bane. He stopped having friends come over because I freaked out anytime someone new came into our house. I'd lock myself away in my room and then have to clean for hours to get rid of any sign of their presence. I knew he didn't exactly understand it, but he also took on the role of my protector.

By the time the new house was finished and I've moved in, Clay had gone away to college. I envied him and the freedoms he had.

14

What must it have been like, with a whole new group of people in a school that had more students than our entire town had citizens? What had he seen? Learned? I couldn't imagine it. Then Mom called and said he would be coming back to town, and that made no sense to me at all. He'd gotten away from here—why come back?

He called me occasionally, and we would talk. I had no problems with phone calls, at least not from Clay. He told me he'd been hired to be the deputy of the county, and how much he looked forward to seeing me. That never happened. As much as I loved Mom and Clay, they were no longer part of my world, and having them in my house would require me to put things back to rights after they were gone. In essence, I'd be excising them from my life each time, and I couldn't handle that. Easier to just not let them visit.

I admit, I was proud of him and what he'd accomplished. Roy Campbell retired several years after the incident—partly because he claimed he never really recovered after what happened to me—and Clay became the youngest sheriff in the state. He had the respect and admiration of the majority of the town for his fair and evenhanded policies, which apparently did not extend to me.

"Fine," I agreed. "If he comes by, I'll talk to him and get his name. But that's it, Clay. I won't do anything else. As soon as I have his name, you promise me you'll ask him to stop running by my house."

"No," Clay replied, his tone harsh. "I've told you, there's no law against running. I can ask him to find another route, but should he say no, I can't force him to stop. If—and I stress, *if*—he threatens you, or you feel honestly unsafe because of his presence, then I'll speak with him."

At the moment I hated him so much, I hung up. I knew it was a childish act, but I needed balance in my life, and even though it would likely take me months to get used to the jogger being gone if he stopped running by, it would be better than trying to come to terms with having him around.

I COULDN'T find it within myself to talk to him for the first four days. I kept hoping he'd stop running by and my life would go back to normal.

I should have known better. Ever since the incident, nothing went the way I expected it to. I continued to watch him, and I had to admit, the apprehension that coursed through me had eased. He didn't really frighten me anymore, but the thought of talking to him filled me with dread. What made it worse for me? He'd continued to glance toward the house, and if he saw me, he'd give a smile or a little wave.

No, I wasn't being honest. After a few weeks of him waving, I had actually started to weave that into my daily routine. I stood in front of the window, looking out at the road every day at ten thirty. One day it rained, and he was thirteen minutes late. I went into panic mode, hyperventilating and pacing around the house, chastising myself. How had he become a part of my world? Why did I now depend on him to be where I expected him to be? I grew angry with myself for that. Despite the pleading I'd done with Clay, I no longer wanted the man to stop running by my house now that I'd grown used to seeing him.

And worse, when he waved, I had started waving back.

Days five and six were spent trying to psych myself up, telling myself it was no big deal. I only had to ask the man his name. How hard could it be?

Morning broke on day seven. My last chance. I'd hedged as long as I could, and now I had to suck it up to keep my brother off my back. Midmorning, I glanced at the clock and saw it was nearly time for him to begin his first pass by my place. I considered waiting for his return trip at eleven forty-five, but I knew if I didn't get this over with, I'd chicken out and then have to deal with Clay.

I stepped outside and took a deep breath. The air had a nip to it now that October had come. The changing leaves were beautiful, all gold and red, falling from the trees to where they would become food for the animals, or to wait for spring so they could become part of the circle of life. I'd stored my canned goods in the root cellar, knowing they'd keep me well-fed when the deep winter snows began to pile around my house, and I would curl up, warm and cozy, in front of the small fireplace in my home.

It struck me then like a bolt from the blue. Winter would be here soon. That meant the jogger wouldn't be coming back this way at least until spring, if ever. After the winter thaws, the roads would be filled with potholes big enough to lose a car in, so why would he want to take that kind of chance? I could feel the tremors in my chest at the thought of my life changing yet again, and I didn't know if I could handle it.

The house beckoned me, offering safety and security. If I went inside and ignored the jogger for the next month or so, I could wean myself away from expecting him, and maybe the separation wouldn't be so bad. As I was taking several steps toward the front door, I heard the slap of feet and the steady inhale and exhale. I turned, and he came into view, and the air got sucked from my lungs. He had on thin shorts and no shirt. He reminded me of the stories of Apollo, the Greek god of the sun. His sweat-slick skin literally shone in the morning light.

As he approached the yard, I stepped toward the fence. He smiled when he saw me and slowed his pace. His chest heaved, and I found myself staring at it. From a distance it had been beautiful, but standing near enough to see droplets of sweat trickling down? Stunning didn't even come close to describing him. He wasn't what I would consider classically handsome. His nose seemed a little small on his face, and his deep-set brown eyes, the same shade as creamed coffee, were spaced just a little far apart. But taken as a whole, he was the most beautiful thing I'd ever seen.

"Good morning," he called as he stopped, still jogging in place.

"Hi," I replied, my voice breaking. "Hi," I said again, a little stronger this time.

"Nice to finally meet you." He held out his hand. "Charlie Carver."

I stared at his hand for a moment before hesitantly reaching for it. His grip was warm and moist. He blushed, drew his hand back, and apologized for his damp grip, wiping his hand on his shorts.

We stood in awkward silence for another moment or two, Charlie glancing around the yard.

"You've got a really nice place here," he said, his tone cheerful and bright. His feet stopped moving, and only the rise of his chest and the sheen of his skin told me that he'd been running just a few minutes before.

I found myself mesmerized by him. He reminded me of a stream of sunlight, coming into the window and falling into my chair, where it warmed me all afternoon.

"So…," he said, "do you have a name, or am I supposed to guess it? Because I have to warn you, I'm not really good at things like that."

His question jolted me out of my reverie and made me remember I was supposed to be uncomfortable in his presence. But I wasn't. I mean, I could feel the twinges of nerves, and part of me still wanted to rush back into the house, but more of me actually felt okay with him.

"Oh, s-s-sorry," I stammered. "Matt. Matt Bowers."

"It's very nice to meet you, Matt Bowers." He waved his hand, gesturing toward the property I worked hard to maintain. "You've got a great place here," he repeated.

I could feel heat rising in my face at his compliment.

Then he aimed a lopsided smile at me, and everything froze. I found myself transported to another time, a different facial expression, and hearing once more the words that had been seared into my mind: *You knew why we were coming out here.* I couldn't draw a breath, and Charlie's expression morphed into a sneer. His beautiful face twisted into an ugly mask. I could see his mouth move but had no idea why. It didn't matter, though.

I turned and ran for the house, slammed the door behind me, and bolted it. I hurried to the bathroom, where I dropped to my knees, ignoring the pain that jolted through my body, and stuck my head in the toilet bowl, expelling my breakfast.

The pounding at the door, and the voice calling my name, only served to heighten my anxiety. When the door jiggled, I screamed, and Charlie's voice rose to a panicked level. He banged harder, but that door had been built to last. He wouldn't get in that way.

My heart hammered, my lungs pleaded for air, and my body shook with remembered fear. I tried for short, slow breaths but found myself unable to calm my shattered nerves. My vision of this place as a safe haven, a place to heal, to find myself again, was gone in an instant. Once more, my fault. I'd let my guard down for a moment, the possibility of being what my mother and brother wanted—of being *normal*—seeming tantalizingly within reach. Then reality showed me the truth. That would never happen, and even trying wasted whatever energy had been expended on it.

It was actually a blessing when I passed out.

CHAPTER THREE

"RELAX, MATT. It's okay."

Clay's voice floated close to my ear. My eyes popped open to see him kneeling next to me, with Charlie looking over his shoulder. They were in my home, somewhere they had no business being. I tried to sit up, but Clay held me in place.

"Stay down. Charlie said you had a panic attack, and I think you need to rest."

"You have to get him out of my house," I croaked. The Sahara wasn't nearly as dry as my mouth.

Clay turned to Charlie. "Can you get him some water?"

Charlie dipped his chin, gave a brief look around, then headed off into the other room.

"You scared the shit out of me. If Charlie hadn't called, I wouldn't have known. I'm so sorry I forced you to do this."

"Should be," I gritted out. "Told you."

Clay gave me a wan smile. "You did."

"Charlie Carver," I whispered.

"He's getting you some water. He'll be back in a minute."

"No. His name. It's Charlie Carver. You said if I found out, you'd leave me alone."

"I don't think you—"

"No!" I snapped, my throat aching. "You promised you'd leave me alone. I want both of you out of my house. Please. Just leave. Go away."

Clay closed his eyes and sucked in a breath. "Matt—"

"I want you gone."

"Here," Charlie said, handing Clay the glass of water. He glanced down at me, and for a moment I thought I saw sadness in his eyes. "I'll be going now."

There was so much hurt on both of their faces, but I couldn't afford to feel bad. I needed them gone. Having them in my house ratcheted up my discomfort, and if they didn't go, I'd be right back in panic mode. Clay stood and offered me a hand, but I didn't take it.

"I don't feel right about this," he said, reaching out to stroke my hair. "Please, at least let me take you to the hospital."

"No," I said sharply. I brushed away his hand as I struggled to stand. And it was a struggle. Weakness permeated my body, making me feel like my bones were made of jelly. I wobbled as I got to my feet, and Clay reached out to me, but I shrugged him off. "Get out. Now."

Clay put the glass down next to me, then turned away, Charlie right behind him. They walked toward the door, which had been cracked when they forced it open. The lock hung limply off the frame.

As soon as they were gone, the crushing need to lie down overwhelmed me, but first I had to check everything. I touched each of my items, running my hands over them, ensuring nothing had been disturbed.

When my needs were satisfied, I picked up the glass my brother had set down, took it to the sink, washed it thoroughly, then put it back up on the shelf. After, I called Mr. Gianetti, the man who I could get just about anything from, about ordering a new door. He assured me he could have it to me within a week. In the meantime I did my best to bar the door. It wasn't perfect, but it was reasonably sturdy. Once that was settled, my mind finally slowed down. Only then could I collapse onto the chair, allow my body to relax, and let sleep come.

THE SHRILL sound of Clay's ringtone woke me a few hours later. Still exhausted, I reached over and picked up the phone. "What?"

"How are you feeling?"

"Like shit," I answered honestly. My head weighed a ton. No way could I lift it off the pillowy cushion. "Did you need something?"

"Just wanted to check on you," he said, his voice soft.

"I'm fine," I lied.

"No, you're not." He sighed. "You know you're a crappy liar."

A deep breath. "Fine. I freaked out. I admit it. But you should have known not to bring him in my house."

Clay grumbled something about ungrateful sons of bitches, then launched into a tirade. "Charlie *helped* me get in so we could check on you. He bruised his shoulder trying to get the door open himself because he was concerned you might need help. He stayed there until I could get to you. And what the hell did you do? You treated him like dirt! He stood there while you told me to get him out of your house."

"But—"

"No buts!" he shouted. "I'm sick to death of your buts and excuses. I don't care how you treat me. I've known you long enough to understand what's going on, but I had to apologize to Charlie, then try to explain to him why you're... you."

"So you went ahead and told him what happened to me?" I shouted as I gripped the arm of the chair. Bad enough my family thought I was a freak. I didn't want Charlie to get that idea in his head. Not that my earlier performance would help dissuade him from that.

"What? God, no. That's not my story to tell. I told him you were antisocial and had been since we were kids."

"So, you're saying he didn't already know who I was?"

"No, he moved here about two years ago. He's a writer, works from home. There are times he leaves town to go on a book tour and I've watered his plants. Charlie came back from the last tour about eight months ago. Since then, he's been working in the library, helping out Mrs. Tennyson. She's told me she hopes he'll take her job when she retires."

"That'll never happen. She's too ornery to retire."

"She's eighty-six. Doesn't see too good out of her right eye. She suffers from dizzy spells, and more than once she's been taken from the library or her home to be checked out for vertigo. The doctors don't know if she has long left."

The last time I went to the library, Mrs. Tennyson had talked to me about getting comics in. She thought more kids would show up if there was something to read that they might enjoy. She loved helping people find what they were looking for or something new. It was her who had given me the dog-eared copy of *My Side of the Mountain*. I'd read that thing hundreds of times since then. The binding had come loose and the pages weren't in the best of shape, but I couldn't get rid of that book. It held a special place in my collection, bound together by frayed rubber bands. At least once a year I would take it down and read it again. I never told anyone, but I came to love Mrs. Tennyson. I saw her as a surrogate grandmother, and though she denied it—probably because she had a reputation for being a grouch—I knew from her fond expressions that she held me in high regard.

She taught me there could be joy found in reading, and I took to it with a passion. *My Side of the Mountain* remained my favorite, but Mrs. Tennyson nudged me in the direction of other classic literature, such as *Twenty Thousand Leagues Under the Sea* and *The Time Machine*. That started my collection of books, ones that remained with me to this day. I found safety in them, comfort when everything else became too overwhelming. Suffice it to say, after the incident I read a lot. Mom had told me Mrs. Tennyson asked after me, but I couldn't go back to the library. She became another in the long list of people I'd failed.

"Tell him…. Tell him I'm sorry, okay?"

"Sure. But you need help, you have to know that."

Yeah, hard to deny it. "When everyone leaves me alone, I'm fine." Weak excuse, but true. Before Charlie came along, I enjoyed the peace and quiet. The memories never seemed so insistent when I had a routine to follow, a good book to read, and the solitude my place afforded me.

"No, you're not. Mom wants to see you. When I told her what happened today, she got into the car to come out there. It wasn't easy, but I convinced her not to come. You're breaking her heart, you know."

Fuck. Why did he have to pile the pressure on? Did he think I didn't know how badly I hurt everyone else? That the memory of my mother's tears as she watched me descend into my own nightmare had faded? Leaving home had been as much for them as for me. I couldn't stand their looks of pity every time I needed to retreat to a safe spot.

"So, what? You're going to go see Hamlin?"

"No, I gave my word. After today, I won't say anything else. Just think about what I've said. Mrs. Tennyson asks about you, Mom wants to see you, and I…." I thought I heard him sniffle, and my stomach clenched. "I want my brother back. I have to go. I won't call you anymore. If you want to talk, I'll be happy to listen, but I can't do this.

I've watched you spiral down the drain my whole life, and I can't sit back and pretend it doesn't hurt. Goodbye, Matt."

"Wait!" I shouted, but he'd already disconnected. My finger poised over the dial pad, ready to call him back, but to what end? I couldn't change who I was any more than he could. Clay didn't see it that way, though. He thought if I tried harder, my world would be sunshine and roses. Even Rob had told me I would always have issues. He could teach me coping methods, but he couldn't make it go away. Who I was now? That was the person I would be for the rest of my life. I had to accept it, but apparently they didn't.

Instead of ruminating on it, I forced myself to get up, trudge to my room, and lie down. I pulled the covers over me and went back to sleep. The problems had been there for thirteen years. I had no doubt they'd still be there tomorrow.

THE SUN streamed through my open bedroom door far too early the next morning. I tried to not open my eyes, but my larks were in good form, warbling away. I glanced over at the clock and wondered once again why I bothered to have one. Almost ten. I hadn't slept so long or hard in years. I pulled the covers up to my chin, rolled over, and tried to go back to sleep. A moment later I sat bolt upright. Almost ten. Would Charlie run by the house today? It seemed unlikely after yesterday, but I slid out of bed and made my way to the window. The urge to be outside to see him clearly tugged at me, but instead I went to the bookcase and grabbed my copy of *My Side of the Mountain*. I took a seat in the chair where I could read in peace but see outside. Not an ideal solution, but it calmed me knowing that I could still see Charlie—assuming he jogged by.

By quarter after, he hadn't passed by the house. I couldn't focus on the words I had intended to read, as one ran into the other. I lost my place so many times, I gave up even trying. Once the rubber band was back in place and the book safely returned to the shelf, I made a circuit through the house, touching everything, before I went outside. A heavy, muggy feeling descended, which left me damp in a matter of moments. Though likely it had been the humidity that kept him from running, my mind still played all manner of games, until I'd convinced myself I had chased him away, which was probably the best for my continued peace. So now that I had what I wanted, why wasn't I happy?

I walked down the path that led to my tiny toolshed and picked up my small spade to turn over the ground in my flower bed. I rounded the corner to the front of the house, knelt down in the rich soil, and began to prepare the ground for winter, making sure I fertilized the area where my bulbs would be placed for their long winter's nap. Yard work always calmed me, made me feel one with the world. After five minutes, I dropped the trowel, then slumped to the ground, unable to concentrate on one of the things that had always brought me peace.

Then I heard the familiar *slap-slap-slap* of rubber soles on the dirt road. My heart raced, though my mind believed it to be an illusion brought about by want. When the staccato beat drew closer and the sounds of panted breaths reached my ears, I stood and headed for the front door. Determined not to allow myself to hope, I decided retreat would be the better option—hide until Charlie left, and then try to find my rhythm again. But I wanted to see him more than I ever thought could be possible. To watch as his chest expanded while it drew in air, to delight in the small brown pebbled nipples, partially hidden beneath a dusting of hair, to remember what desire felt like. It didn't matter if Charlie was gay or straight. He was the first real man I'd seen in the flesh, and I enjoyed the view. His body was so unlike that of the developing guys in the shower. It held curves and planes that aroused me and made me wonder what else lay hidden beneath his skimpy shorts.

After the incident, my body really didn't respond like it used to. Before that, a stiff breeze would cause a stiffness of my own. Fortunately we had two bathrooms in the house, because I spent a lot of time in one of them. Then Mr. Jackson happened. After that, I rarely had an erection, and when I did, it seldom lasted. Sixteen years old, and I should have had callouses on my hand. Instead I had memories of a smell that permeated my mind, which killed my mood better than a dozen cold showers. When I'd seen Charlie, though? God, the ache in my balls reminded me of how long it had been since I touched myself for anything other than washing or using the bathroom.

He rounded the bend, and I couldn't breathe. My legs refused to work, despite the fact that I willed them to run. Instead they held me hostage as he neared my property. His hand went up a little, then dropped to his side. He turned his gaze to the road, watching his feet. Tight bands encircled my chest and squeezed. I'd done that to him, made him uncertain, unsure if being friendly would be the wrong thing to do.

And while it went against everything in me, I said, "Hello."

He stopped, still maintaining a slow cadence as he cooled down. "Hey, Matt. I… is it okay if I'm here?" Charlie asked, a slight quaver in his voice.

Was it? He'd certainly made himself a part of my world. Seeing him today had calmed an ache in my stomach because I'd expected him to be there. Hell, I *needed* him to be there for my own peace of mind.

"You're late," I snapped, a lot more harshly than I'd intended.

He smiled sheepishly. "Yeah, I had to go to the library today. I did a reading for six lovely women who I think I might have scandalized with my writing. I had to stop, because I thought Mrs. Patterson was having heart palpitations. And then afterward, I had to make a trip to the hardware store."

Clay had said Charlie wrote. "What do you write?"

"Murder mysteries," he replied. He must have noted the confusion in my expression, because he gave me a little smirk. "The main character is gay."

Oh. *Oh!* "You're gay?" I immediately regretted my tone, because it sounded accusatory.

"Yeah," he answered sheepishly. "Is that a problem?"

"No, not at all." Hell no. My heart did a little jig, and my cock actually twitched.

"Good. So what about you? Do you have a girlfriend? Boyfriend?"

I shook my head. "No, no one."

That brought a big smile to his face. "Really?" He sounded so happy.

I took two steps toward him, and the tightness in my chest receded as I got closer. "So… about yesterday…."

25

He nodded. "Panic attack? I get it. I have those when I have to do a reading. Don't worry about it. But if you'd like to tell me what set it off, I'll try not to repeat whatever I did to cause it."

He thought *he* had caused it. "You didn't do anything," I promised. "This started way before you."

Charlie tilted his head a little, then flashed me a cheeky grin. "If you offer me something to drink, I'll forgive you."

My heart thudded. Did he think I'd let him in my house? Because no way would that happen. Still, if he wanted to sit outside….

"I made some lemonade," I told him. "It's probably not what you're used to. I have a few trees I've grown over the years in my hothouse."

"You grow your own trees? That's… wow. I don't know anyone who does something like that."

"Most of the things I eat are what I plant and harvest. I like to work the soil." Not a lie, but not the whole truth. Still, how long would it be before Charlie heard my story?

"I'd love some lemonade, if you don't mind." He pointed to the swing on my front porch. It was one of my favorite pieces of furniture, great for wrapping myself up and snuggling in for a while to take in the beauty of the land. There was a small table next to it, and across from it sat a really nice chair. Both the swing and the chair had extra thick cushions that you just sank into. "Is it okay if I sit and talk with you while I drink?"

My pulse sped up a little. An internal war raged, part of me wanting him to leave and part of me wanting him to stay so I could get to know him better. While I hated people on my property, Charlie's quirky smile, runner's body, and the fact that he wrote actual books meant something to me. Sucking in a deep breath, I uttered words I never thought I'd hear myself say.

"Sure. Have a seat, and I'll get you a glass."

CHAPTER FOUR

"So THEN the detective says, 'I knew you were guilty the day you walked into my office. The stench dripped from you like so much rotting garbage.' And the killer says, 'Then why did you take the case?' And Tremaine answers, 'Because I needed to find evidence that you were guilty, so I could have you arrested for murdering your brother. Basically you paid to have me get you put on death row.'"

I was hooked on his words. I had never heard of his books, but now I wanted to know more. I glanced down at my watch and realized I had been sitting with him on my porch for nearly three hours. I'd never spent that much time with any other person after the incident. And I didn't feel freaked out by his presence. After seeing him every day, he'd somehow become a fixture, and that desperate need to keep order in my life had somehow come to include him. I wasn't ready to let him into my home, but I found I didn't mind talking to him so much.

"Wow," I said, knowing that it wasn't nearly what I meant.

"You've seriously never read one of my books?" He seemed amused.

"No. I… I don't get out much."

He chuckled. "I'm teasing you. My niche is pretty small, but if you like mysteries…."

"I do love to read," I admitted.

"If you give me your email, I'll send you copies. I mean, if you think they're worth reading."

Yes, I wanted to read them. I'd never even heard of a book that had a gay character, but to have six books in a series where the detective had a lover—which Charlie said would lead to a proposal soon—and they lived together? That sounded amazing. Most of my books were young adult stories that Mrs. Tennyson had given me. After the incident, I took those with me. I hadn't purchased any others because they would disturb everything I had. But now I wanted to read Charlie's work.

"I don't have email," I replied. "I don't even have a computer."

He grinned, which did strange things to my stomach. "So you really are roughing it, huh?"

No condemnation, just a simple fact. "I am. I love it out here. In the summer I can stretch out in the grass and watch the stars overhead. They shine so bright, and you can see forever in them. Then the lightning bugs come out. I get two shows for the price of one. Flashing lights dancing against a solid backdrop of stars. It's an amazing place to live." And until that very moment, I hadn't realized how lonely it was. Talking with Charlie had shown me that my desire to be alone might keep my head clear, but it also caused my heart to ache.

"I can understand that," Charlie assured me. "When I left New York to come to Fall Harbor, everyone thought I must have gone around the bend." He tapped his finger on the arm of the swing. "To leave where my publisher was to come to a Podunk town no one had ever even heard of? Can't say I blame them."

There were questions I wanted to ask, but I wasn't sure how appropriate they were. Naturally, I blurted out the most important one anyway. "So why'd you come here, of all places?"

He got a pained expression, but it vanished so quickly, I thought maybe I'd been mistaken. "I had a lover. His name was Mitch. I honestly thought we'd be together forever. Us writers, we believe in happily ever after. Apparently Mitch didn't share my dreams. I went out on a tour one week and was scheduled to be gone for six days. They'd scheduled several readings at a popular gay bookstore in San Francisco. Me and four other authors were supposed to take part throughout the week. My agent said this would be good exposure for the series since it was doing great in sales. Plus it would give me a chance to meet some well-respected authors, maybe pick up a few tips to help hone my craft.

"Well, the shop where they were holding the reading had some pipes burst and a lot of water damage. They were unable to find a venue on such short notice, so they cancelled the event with the promise to schedule another one at a later date. I caught the red-eye flight home, expecting to have the week with Mitch."

Charlie paused and swiped his hand across his eyes. When he continued, his voice sounded hoarse and scratchy. "Thing of it was, I'd had an engagement ring hidden in my drawer for about two months. I figured this week would be the time to do it. So all the way home, I planned how I'd ask him to share my life. I'd sweep into the house we owned, grab him, and we'd fly to Maine to get married on the steps of a beautiful B and B I found that overlooked a field of wildflowers. I had my assistant make all the arrangements."

He stopped talking then, and I had the urge to take his hand or hug him. Something. Because I could see the pain clearly etched on his face. Of course, I didn't move.

"You don't have to—"

He smiled again, but it wasn't as warm as it had been previously. "No, it's okay. I don't mind. Do you think I could have a little more lemonade? It's really very good." He gave me a sheepish grin. "I mean, if it's not inconvenient."

It would be his third glass, and the fact that he said how delicious it was made me feel good. Being able to share something I'd made, knowing it had been enjoyed, gave me tiny flutters in my chest.

"Sure, no problem at all."

I picked up his glass, took it inside, and washed it. Then I pulled a clean glass from the cabinet, filled it to the brim, and walked back out onto the porch. Charlie sat back, his arm over his eyes.

"You okay?" I asked, putting the glass down on the small table next to him.

He sat up straighter and smiled. "Yeah, actually I am." He picked up the lemonade, took a healthy swig, then put it back down. "Okay, so where was I? Oh yeah. Okay. I had everything planned out, down to the last detail. We'd have tickets waiting for us at the counter when we got to the airport, so all I needed to do was walk in, kiss Mitch, tell him to get packed, and we'd be on our way. I walked in at two thirty in the morning with this big smile on my face, put my bags down, then tiptoed to our bedroom to surprise him. The happiness I'd felt all the way home promptly fell away when I saw him, the man who told me he never bottomed, on his hands and knees, being fucked by one of our friends."

I must have gasped because he pinned me with a stare.

"I know, right?" He huffed a breath. "I couldn't believe what I was seeing. Well, really, all I saw were my plans going down the drain."

"What did you do?"

He gave me such a sad, tight smile, I felt I had no choice. I reached over and put my hand on top of his. We'd shaken hands before, but this time it had an intimacy to it I hadn't expected. I won't deny how difficult touching him was. I had to keep reminding myself it wasn't wrong to comfort a friend, which led to me wondering when I'd started thinking of Charlie as a friend. But I didn't break contact with him, which made me proud.

Charlie shrugged. "In the blink of an eye, everything became clear to me. The man I thought would be my home, my life, no longer had a place in it. Since my luggage from my trip was sitting by the door, I went back, picked it up, and caught a cab to the airport, where I retrieved the ticket, and here I am."

"Did you ever talk to him again?"

"He called me about a week later when I didn't come back after the tour. He acted all worried, said he missed me terribly and thought something had happened. I asked if that came before or after Scott fucked him. He didn't say anything for a few moments. Then he told me he had needed Scott because I was always busy and never had time for him. I was either writing or on tour, and it didn't seem like he was important in my life. Scott was there for him when I wasn't."

"It wasn't your fault!" I shouted, then covered my mouth.

Charlie gave me a grin. "Wow, you're a tiger, aren't you?" He looked down at our hands, then back at me. "I never thought it was my fault. Mitch had been invited to come along on the trips but always said he had other things to do. It wasn't like he couldn't take time off. I make good money, so he didn't need to work. He kept the condo clean, did the shopping, and things like that. It took me a year of being here to realize that we hadn't been lovers so much as client and cleaning boy. With the blessing of distance, I found that the feelings I thought I had, I'd overromanticized in my head. The other curse of writing, you know."

I didn't. I had no idea what to say to him to make it better. I couldn't even be sure that was possible. "I'm sorry," I said sincerely.

He sat back and grinned at me. I immediately regretted the loss of contact, which seemed weird to me. "Nothing to be sorry for, I promise. Originally I thought being here would just be a vacation. I figured I'd pull myself back together, then return to New York and carry on with my life there. But this place has a way of getting a grip on you. Most people don't seem to have a problem with me being gay, though there was a couple who approached me in the restaurant to assure me they didn't care as long as I didn't flaunt it. Oh, did I mention they were holding hands at the time?"

A very inelegant snort burst from me that had Charlie quirking a brow, then laughing so loud the birds scattered from the trees. My gaze went to the horizon, where I could see the long shadows creeping up. I hadn't realized it had gotten so late. Charlie must have noticed where I was looking, because he stood.

"I'm sorry to have kept you from your yard work. It's been a while since I had such a nice conversation."

I wanted to tell him to stay. I didn't want him to stop talking. But he had a life in town that I couldn't be a part of. "Thank you for coming by. I'm sorry you had to stop your run."

He waved a hand dismissively. "I run every day. I can afford to take a break." He looked down at his shuffling feet. "Do you think maybe I could come back tomorrow? I'd really like... more lemonade."

His innocent expression had me chuckling. "Yeah, I'll have to make some more, but I'll save you some."

"Sounds great. I'll even bring some supplies to fix your door, if you want."

Shock coursed through me. Usually I was so anal about everything, but I hadn't even thought about the door since we started talking. My hands shook a little at the realization that my routine had been disrupted and it hadn't bothered me as much as I thought it would.

In fact, I hadn't even given it a thought while Charlie was here. He occupied my mind and engaged me in spirited conversation. I actually enjoyed talking to him.

I should have known it wouldn't last.

31

THAT NIGHT as I lay in bed, I reached down and touched my cock. I gave it a few tentative strokes, wanting to see if maybe it would do what a dick should do. It didn't. It sat there, flaccid, as it usually did. I tried picturing Charlie in my mind. His body, his voice, his smile. Still nothing. Frustrated, I rolled over, punched my pillow a few times, and tried to sleep. Instead I ran our conversation over and over in my head. He had somehow slipped past my defenses, made me enjoy spending time with him, luxuriating in his attention. His voice, deep and sultry, held me spellbound. I could understand why people came to see him read.

That set me off on another tangent. What would he be like in his element? Sitting in front of an audience, holding court. He'd already admitted he had issues with panic attacks, but obviously they hadn't prevented him from doing his job. I let my imagination wander, picturing myself in a bookstore when Charlie strode in, smooth and confident. He'd smile at me and take a seat. He'd toss out a few quips to get the audience ready, but his attention never wavered from me. When he read, the words were meant for me alone. He captured me with nothing more than the sound of his voice, which kept me mesmerized as he told his story. It didn't matter what he read, though. Only that he didn't stop.

I let my fingers drift down my stomach and through my pubic thatch until I reached my cock, which stood up tall and proud. I wrapped my fingers around the straining shaft, the memory of how good it felt coming back to me.

Then everything went haywire. I heard a noise outside, remembered the door, and realized I wasn't safe. Anyone could walk into my house. I knew how ludicrous it sounded, because other than the deliveries for the things I ordered online, and Charlie now running the road, no one had come onto my property in years. But in my excitement, Mr. Jackson's image loomed large in my mind, half-remembered nightmares that woke me in a cold sweat reminding me I wasn't truly safe. I could picture the lock, and the fear reared up, threatened to consume me. My erection wilted, gone like snow under the summer sun. I bolted out of bed, dressed, and went to the door.

My brother and Charlie had done a number on the damn thing. While I'd purchased the sturdiest bolt I could find, which stayed in one piece, the door had been another matter entirely. Splintered wood stood up from where the lock had been. I grabbed my tools from the closet and set to trying to repair the damage. Of course the whole thing turned out to be futile. There would be no fixing this mess. I'd ordered the new one, but it would still be days before it showed up. My heart seized at thoughts I couldn't control. Mr. Jackson was no longer in prison. Clay had said he'd moved to Alabama, but what if he'd come back? He could be outside, hiding in the dark. What would I do if he were there? Panic began to well up inside me.

Staying alone in the house, unprotected, had me rushing around, touching all of my things. I had been self-sufficient for years, never needing anyone for anything. I prided myself on my independence. I'd been a modern-day version of Sam Gribley. Now? My gut churned at the thought someone could come into my house.

I hurried back into the bedroom and grabbed my phone from the nightstand. I hated that I needed to do this, but in this case, fear had become the perfect motivation. My hands shook so hard I couldn't be sure I had even dialed the right number until a gruff voice, rough from sleep, answered with a snarled, "Hello?"

"Clay?" I asked, even though I knew it was him. "Clay, please. I need you." I couldn't keep the quiver from my voice.

And immediately he was awake. "Where are you? What's wrong?"

"My door is broken," I sobbed.

Clay growled his reply. "Yeah, I said I was sorry."

"No," I whispered, squeezing my eyes shut. "I'm alone and… I'm afraid."

Terrified would be more appropriate. I could see shadows outside, and every one of them reached for me, wanted to grab me.

"Matt?" He sounded concerned, but also authoritative. "Listen to me. I'm on my way, okay? Just stay there and I'll get to you in fifteen minutes."

I knew better. At minimum it would be almost thirty. But I needed him. The terror of being alone, unsafe, overrode all other fears. "Please," I begged.

33

He disconnected, and I went into the bedroom, closed the door, hid in the corner, and stared at the clock.

Twelve minutes later, I heard the faint wail of a siren, and I knew Clay was coming. I slumped in relief when I heard him calling my name. I got up and rushed outside to meet him. He opened his arms, and I threw myself into them, burying my face in his chest. He held me to him, his fingers sliding through my hair. He was whispering, promising me I had nothing to be afraid of. I let him hold me, something I hadn't let anyone do since the incident. I took comfort in his touch, his voice. He led me to the porch, sat me down, and held me until the tremors stopped.

A few moments later, I heard a truck, and I tried to stand, the fear making a resounding comeback. Clay held tight, reminding me everything was okay. When the headlights turned down the road, I clung to him. I had no rational explanation for my fears.

The vehicle came to a screeching halt, and the door burst open. When a man stepped out, Clay stood and called to the occupant, "We're on the porch."

A figure came around the side, and I had no idea who it could be until he stepped in front of the headlights. "Charlie," I whimpered.

"I came as quick as I could. I brought what you asked for, Clay."

They went to the back of the truck and lifted something from it. It took me a moment before I could understand what I saw. A door, and a pretty heavy one, if the huffs and puffs from the two men were any indication.

"Matt, we have to go inside. Is that going to be a problem?"

The urge to tell them to leave the door and I'd hang it myself almost overrode common sense. Clay and Charlie were big men, much larger than me. If they were having trouble hefting the door, how in the hell would I be able to do it myself? I nodded to my brother.

"No, you need to tell me. Is us going in there going to be an issue?"

"Yes," I whispered, my fists clenched tightly at my sides. "But I need you to do it."

"Okay."

They went straight to it, removed the old door, then installed the new. I marveled at the way they worked together, Clay taking charge and making the process swift. The new door was much heavier than the one that had come with the house, and that added security calmed me. I could lock myself away again. I could....

"Clay?"

He glanced up from what he was doing, the hammer in his hand ready to tap at the hinge pins. "Hmm?"

"Thank you."

He smiled at me, then went back to his task. It took them several hours to get everything done right, but when they finished, I breathed easier.

"Do you want some lemonade?" I asked.

Clay smiled, wide and genuine. "Nah, but thanks. I have to work in a few hours."

It struck me then. Clay, the one who had just told me he wouldn't call me again, had gotten up in the middle of the night, dragged Charlie with him, and come to my remote home because I'd been afraid.

"Thank you," I whispered, overcome with emotion.

Clay reached out to touch me, but then let his hand drop. "It's what brothers do," he informed me. "If you ever need me, you call, and I'll come running."

"Same goes for me," Charlie told me. "When Clay said you needed help, I didn't even think about why. I came." He stretched and yawned. "But now I need to get some sleep. Though I normally work the afternoon shift, the other librarian needed off, so I'm opening the library tomorrow."

These two men humbled me. Clay had proved to me that despite my problems, he would be there for me. And Charlie? Charlie showed he didn't care about the why—he only saw a friend in need. I wanted desperately to hug them both, to thank them. Instead I walked them to their trucks and we said goodbye.

After they left, I had to touch everything in my house twice. Their presence had been welcome in the dark of the night, but still it unnerved me. I sat in the kitchen, staring at the new door. The red-and-white paint job went surprisingly well with my decor. More importantly, the solidness made me feel far safer in my home than I had before.

And I had my brother to thank.

CHAPTER FIVE

I CRASHED hard after I calmed myself down nearly an hour later. The past couple of days had taken their toll on me, both physically and mentally. Everything I believed, all the things I'd told myself I needed to keep me safe, had been called into question by a late-night phone call and the response it got.

Wearing nothing but a smile, I got out of bed and went to the kitchen for a glass of lemonade. I really, really wanted coffee, but I found that when I drank too much caffeine, my anxiety went through the roof. I cut that out of my life right away, though I still had decaf on occasion. Sugar wasn't so bad as long as I didn't overdo it. And I loved my lemonade. To me it had the perfect blend of tartness and sweetness. Just enough to give it pucker power. Deciding to give Sam Gribley another try, I slipped on some clothes, grabbed my favorite book, and headed for the porch, stopping to run my fingers over the work Charlie and Clay had done. The place felt safe again. Then I remembered I had asked Mr. Gianetti to order me a door. I thought about calling to cancel, but after this, I figured I could keep it in storage in case I ever needed one.

As soon as the door opened, I knew it would be a beautiful day. The air had a fall crispness to it that would fade over the course of the morning, warming to a beautiful Indian summer. I had very few chores to do, and I didn't usually start on those until about two, so I thought I had time to read until then. The swing welcomed me like an old friend as I sank into it, providing me with warmth and comfort.

About twenty minutes later, the sound of rubber on dirt caught my attention, and I sat up straight, every nerve on full alert. Not only was it too early for Charlie, but he'd been here only a few hours ago. He'd also said he had to open the library, so it couldn't be him coming down the way.

"Just me, Matt!" Charlie yelled a few moments before coming into view.

The breath whooshed from my lungs. I rushed inside and put the book back on the shelf, then returned to the porch in time to see Charlie as he came around the bend, a big smile on his face. He was shirtless, and I suppressed a moan at seeing his chest. He had a gray T-shirt tucked into the pocket of his running shorts, which made me wonder if he'd taken it off just for me. When he coughed, I realized I had been thinking too hard and felt my cheeks heat. He stood at the gate and grinned.

"Did you want to sit?" I asked as I took my seat and picked up the now-empty glass. I rolled it in my hands, focusing on the coolness. "Sorry, I didn't think you would be here so early."

"Yes, as a matter of fact, I do," he answered, a wide grin on his face. He pushed open the gate and sauntered up to where I sat. Without saying anything, he opened the bag he'd slung over his shoulder and reached inside. When he pulled out a stack of books, I gave him a curious look. "You said you'd like to read them. I had paperback copies at home, so I thought you might want them."

When I didn't move, his expression slipped a little. I wanted to take them, but they didn't belong in my house. I kept trying to tell myself that the gift from Charlie shouldn't be an issue, but it was and I didn't know why.

He stood for a moment, then coughed. "Okay, how about if I set them down, and if you want to read them, you can? No pressure, honest."

He put them next to where I sat. I glanced down at the cover of the top one. Two men in an intimate pose, one shielding the other. The picture appeared grainy, like something you'd see on old television shows. I guess it had to do with the genre. The title, *Death Comes to Allerton*, had been emblazoned across the top, with a review snippet from the *Literary Times Gazette* that promised it to be a thrill ride like no other. On the bottom of the book, the name Charles Magnus was displayed in a stylish font.

I quirked an eyebrow. "Charles Magnus?"

He blushed and glanced down at his hand. "Pen name. Charlie Carver seemed too blah, my publicist said."

"I think it's a nice name," I told him. Then I realized what I'd said. "For an author, I mean."

37

That devilish smirk flashed across his face. "Sure, for an author," he teased. "So, since you have signed copies of my books, does that entitle me to a lemonade?"

I made a face. "You think my lemonade is only worth some books?"

That brought a laugh. "You're right. My apologies," he said, crossing his right arm over his stomach and giving a slight bow.

I flashed back on the image of him and Clay hanging the door, his tight muscles straining as they worked, the look of sheer determination on his face. He never questioned, never complained. Three in the morning, and he had come out to help Clay. That entitled him to a lot more than lemonade.

"Have a seat. I'll get you something to drink. If you'd rather, I do have coffee. Well, decaf. I don't do well with caffeine."

He waved his hand. "I'd love lemonade, but if we ever decide to have coffee, I'm fine with whatever you've got. Some writers live off caffeine. Me? I can take it or leave it."

"One glass of Matt's special lemonade coming up," I said, trying to give him a smile. I picked up my empty glass and carried it back into the house.

The pitcher in the refrigerator had enough for a glass or two, and it would take me some time to make fresh, which had been my plan for the afternoon. After I washed out the glass I'd used and dried it off, I poured lemonade for him, put the remainder back, and grabbed a glass of water for myself. When I got outside, I found him writing something in one of the books. When he saw me, he closed it quickly, set it back on the pile, put the pen in his bag, and held out his hand.

"Thank you," he said, taking the glass from me. He drained it all in a few gulps, then wiped a hand over the back of his mouth. "You could bottle this stuff. It's way better than what they serve at the Clover."

My cheeks heated at his compliment. "I had a friend who worked there once, and she said they only use a powder mix." I sat in the swing, across from the chair Charlie occupied. He put his glass down, crossed his legs, and stared at me. I squirmed under his scrutiny.

"Is the door working okay?" he asked.

"Y-yes," I stuttered. I wanted to run and hide in my bed when I noticed the way his gaze bored into me. It seemed as though he could see right through me. I couldn't decide if it should be comforting or terrifying.

"Can we talk about last night?" he asked, after what seemed like an eternity.

This had been the second time he'd seen me at my worst. To be honest it surprised me that he had come back at all after getting a call from Clay about a crazy man.

"Hey, how did you know to get here last night?" I asked, hoping to deflect his questions.

"Your brother and I are kinda friends. Okay, really, we're more of acquaintances. I met him one day when he came into the library while I looked around. You can always tell a lot about a town by the books they have. Anyway, he welcomed me to town, told me a little about the history. Asked if my vacation was going well. At first I thought he was being nosey, but then I realized he genuinely wanted to help me find things that might interest me.

"If I had to point to one thing that convinced me to stay here, it would be the feeling of kinship in the town. Like the people in the town all look out for one another. After I returned home, I found that Mitch had moved out. So I sold my place in New York and bought one here. I made the move and haven't regretted it since. I started working at the library, and one day Clay came in. We started talking, and I mentioned that I like to run. His eyes went wide, and he asked me where. I told him. He didn't know you were on my jogging route, and when he found out, it surprised him. We don't really hang out, but I like to think we're somewhat close. When he called and said you were in trouble and needed a hand, I came to help."

It made sense in a weird way. But....

"If you have a truck, why do you jog down my road?"

Charlie sat back and gave me an amused expression. "Your road? I'm sorry, I didn't see the sign that said it led to Matt's Manor."

I dropped my head against the chair and groaned. "Sorry. I might be a little territorial."

"S'okay," he answered. "I come this way because I won't see anyone else from town. I park down the road about three miles, then make my way up here, around the bend, and back. Round-trip it's about seven miles or so."

I sat up and glared at him. "But this area really isn't meant for running."

"That's what makes it so perfect," he countered. "No one else runs here, so I can be lost in my own thoughts. Hell, I was surprised to find someone lived out here."

He had a point. Most folks didn't live this far from town, and those who did owned large tracts of land that they farmed. My house sat on about twenty acres, mostly wooded. It had a pond that was fed by a nearby lake, which provided me with ample opportunity to fish. So with the exception of the area my house and greenhouse took up, I had plenty of room to be by myself. In fact, my nearest "neighbor" was a few miles away.

"I thought you were at the library today," I said, wanting to get back to a safe topic.

He grinned at me, and my stomach fluttered. "I switched with Mrs. Tennyson. I told her I had something I really had to do."

"Oh? What are you going to be doing?"

He laughed. It was a nice laugh, full of life and happiness. "I came to see you, doofus. I wanted to make sure you were okay after last night. Or this morning." He shrugged. "Whatever. And I realized I told you to call me, but I never gave you my number. That's what I wanted to talk to you about."

"Oh, it's okay—"

He held up a hand. "It's not, Matt. I know about panic. Sometimes all you need to get through it is a friendly voice. Other times a hug might be the ticket. I'm not saying it will make all the panic go away. I don't know what causes it for you, but that's not the important thing. What is, at least to me and Clay, is that you have someone you can reach out to when you need to. You live out here, in the quiet and solitude, but you're never alone. Remember that."

The thought of being in Charlie's embrace filled my mind and gave me a strange feeling in my chest. I likened it to what it felt like when Clay

40

held me last night. Safety. I couldn't process it logically. I never needed or wanted anyone to touch me. Last night, though? I sought it out, shocked by how good it felt to be held again. The warmth and comfort I got from Clay kept the fear—all the fears—at bay for a short time.

"Thank you," I replied softly. Charlie really seemed too good to be true. He gazed at me with kindness and what I thought might be affection. Warmth flooded through me when I realized at some point I had mostly stopped being afraid of Charlie and accepted him as part of my world. One of the biggest problems I had hinged on new situations. When whatever I couldn't grow on my own had to be delivered, I needed to touch each item several times, then put it aside where I could become used to it before I could actually put it into storage.

Charlie stood and wiped his hand off on his shorts. "Okay, well, I'd better get back to the library. I promised I'd be there before noon to take over. Remember what I said, Matt. If you ever need help, call someone, okay?"

I got up, but before I could answer, he turned and went to the gate, opened it, looked back and gave a quick wave, then started off down the road. I watched until he was out of sight. I looked down at the table where he had left the books. I admit, I really wanted to read them. I should have been put off by the fact that they were new in the house, but they'd been a gift from Charlie. I had reservations, but I didn't think he would hurt me. I sat on the swing, reached over, and picked up the first one. Opening the cover, I saw what Charlie had written there, and smiled.

It takes courage to ask for help. Thank you for trusting me last night. He'd also written his phone number.

The warmth of tears on my cheeks didn't surprise me. I'd always known my emotions were close to the surface, which probably accounted for a lot of the overwhelming sensations I dealt with. Today I tamped them down, determined to trust Charlie. After all, it was just a book.

THREE HOURS later, I closed the cover and sagged onto the seat. I'd never known someone could write like Charlie had. The level of violence stunned me, but it didn't come across as gratuitous. Every act fit into the story, drove it on. In two hundred pages, he made me laugh, cry, cringe, and worry about the protagonist in a way that almost made him seem real. Even though I had an inkling about the ending, thanks to Charlie's telling me about the book, it still came as a total shock when the detective watched the man die and did nothing to save him.

Donald Tremaine could be a coldhearted bastard, except when it came to Lucien James, his lover. He protected him with a ferocity that overwhelmed me, even though Lucien proved perfectly capable of protecting himself. But when they went to bed together, Lucien gave himself over, and Donald took what he wanted—what he needed—though he did it with love. And it wasn't just said. I could feel it in everything they did for each other.

I picked up the stack of books and took them in the house, placed them on the shelf with my very favorite stories, then glanced over at the clock and groaned.

My chores needed to be done or I would have dived into the second book immediately. *Murder in Times Squared* looked to be even better than *Death Comes to Allerton*. The cover had two crossed knives, dripping with blood. I could make out a shadowy figure in the background, but any details were kept temptingly out of reach. I really wanted to read this book, because Donald had two murders to deal with. They both had similarities, but his main suspect had been miles away from the site where the body had been found, so there was no way he could have done it. I kept looking from the book to the clock. It wouldn't be the end of the world if I didn't rake leaves and mulch them today. They'd still be there tomorrow, I told myself.

But it would seriously disrupt my schedule. The same one I'd adhered to for years. Nothing bad would happen, I tried to convince myself. When the fear welled up, for the first time I pushed against it. It had controlled my life for so long, cost me too much, and I had grown tired of it. I wanted to be me again. The kid who, at thirteen, ran naked through gym class on a dare. The one who wanted to take Marty Hendricks for a drive and park with him, just to see where it would lead. The one who could look at a man and feel something that wasn't fear. I just wanted to be normal again.

Today I would prove to myself that I wasn't a slave to my schedule. I could do this. I took the book back down from the shelf, poured a glass of ice water, and went to sit down so I could once again immerse myself in Donald's world. At first I had problems focusing. My gaze would stray to the leaves that waited to be raked, think about the plants in the greenhouse that needed water and the compost that had to be added today. But I kept at it. I forced myself to read and did indeed start getting into the story. When I snuck a peek at my watch, it had just passed three, and I jumped up. I put the book down and raced to do the chores I'd neglected for an hour. Mentally I berated myself, but inside I felt a glow of pride, because even though it had only been sixty minutes, it was still more than I'd ever done in the past. And maybe that was the key. Doing a little bit at a time, not trying to get everything in my life right at once.

As I spread the fertilizer on the plants, I made a vow to myself that I would try harder. I would do my best to work past one thing each day that caused my anxiety to flare. Not forever, because I didn't think that possibility would ever happen, but like I had done today, I would do it again tomorrow. Maybe one day I would work my way up to two hours. Then maybe a full day.

And tomorrow it would start with Charlie.

AS SOON as I heard the larks the next morning, I hustled out of bed and hurried to the bookcase. Books one and two had been incredible. I'd stayed up way later than I should have to find out who the killer—or should I say, killers—were. It left me breathless. Book three, *The Corpse Wore Death*, beckoned to me. So at five o'clock I sat on the porch, glass of water beside me, poring over the book. It opened with an intense sex scene, which turned out to be the cover for the murder. I shivered at the descriptions Charlie used when the killer went ballistic on his prey, because they were so damned vivid they made me glad I hadn't read them the night before.

I finished just before ten and couldn't wait to see Charlie. He'd be amazed when I told him I'd gotten through three of his books and couldn't wait to tear into the fourth one. I got up, poured the last glass of lemonade for him, quickly made a fresh batch, just in case he wanted more, then went back out onto the porch.

Ten o'clock came and went. Ten thirty. Eleven. Noon.

My pulse quickened. He'd never been this late before, and my mind went over the possibilities. Maybe he'd been called into the library. Or he could have overslept because he'd been up late and gotten up too early the day before. But no matter what I told myself, none of those seemed plausible.

Panic gripped me, and I had no idea what to do. I tried calling his number, but it went to his voicemail. My voice shook horribly when I left a message. Then I recalled what he'd said about Clay. Being the sheriff, maybe Clay might know what was going on. His phone rang three times before he answered.

"Matt," he breathed. "You okay?"

"Yes. No. No, I'm not." I slid my hand through my hair as I struggled to maintain control. A battle I wouldn't win. "I can't get in touch with Charlie, and he hasn't been by today. He comes by every day, but he didn't today, and I'm worried."

I heard him groan.

"What's wrong?" I demanded. "I can hear it in your voice. Something's wrong."

"There was an accident yesterday morning."

CHAPTER SIX

I BURST out laughing. I mean, Clay had done some mean stuff when we were growing up, but this was taking a joke way too goddamn far.

"Matt?"

I squeezed the phone as hard as I could. "Stop fucking lying to me!" I screamed. "Where's Charlie?"

"I'm not lying, honey," he soothed, his voice pitched low like he was talking to a mad dog. "I wish I were. His truck went off the road about four miles down from your place. Dale Jensen saw him go over the embankment. He went down about thirty feet, then hit a tree. I'm sorry, but Charlie's in the hospital."

I couldn't draw a breath to speak. He'd been on his way home after dropping off the books. It was my fault. I did this to him. I—

"It's not your fault, Matthew," Clay snapped.

There was no way to be certain if he knew me that well or if I had been rambling out loud. Either way, it didn't matter. Trepidation filled my heart. I dreaded asking my next question, because if Clay didn't give me a good answer, I would crumble into pieces, and this time I didn't think anyone could put me back together. "Is he okay?"

You could have cut the tension with a knife. Clay stayed quiet too long, so I knew something bad had happened.

"He was lucky his airbag went off," Clay said. "That probably saved his life."

His attempt to placate me did no good. I could feel myself sliding over the precipice. My entire body shook at the thought of Charlie dying, alone at the bottom of the ravine. The images seared my brain, and it hurt to take in air. "Please, Clay…."

He cleared his throat. "I need you to breathe, Matt. Listen to what I'm telling you. He's hurt, but he'll be okay. He broke a couple ribs and his right leg, he's got burns on his face, and he fractured one of his hands. He's okay, though. Do you understand me, Matt? He's going to be fine."

I blew out a breath. I attempted to focus on him saying Charlie would be okay. "What's going to happen to him?"

He hedged again. I hated it when he did that.

"His sister is coming down in a couple days to take him back to New York," he answered slowly.

New York? No! I'd come to the decision that I wanted to try to be a better person, to see if maybe Charlie would... what? Overlook my weirdness? Yes, goddammit. That's exactly what the dream had been. I wanted him to like me, even though I might not be his type. For the first time in years, I finally felt something that wasn't fear or hurt or anger. I wanted to rage against the injustice, against how fucking unfair it was. Instead I simply said, "Oh."

"I'm sorry, Matt. So truly sorry. I thought—"

There wasn't anything left to say. I hung up the phone, then ignored it when it started ringing again. For months I wanted to get rid of Charlie, make him go away so he couldn't scare me. Now I found that him leaving frightened me even more. I'd be alone again. I fucking hated being alone.

I threw myself on the bed, tears staining my cheeks. I'd always thought of myself as strong because I didn't need anyone. The lies we tell ourselves are the most damning ones of all, because after a time we start to believe them. The truth had always been too terrible to contemplate. My fears controlled me. It wasn't what my teacher had done to me. Sure, he might have put me in the cell, but I'd locked the door behind me and thrown away the damn key. I had never been strong, not once since the incident. And though the idea forming in my head scared me to death, I *would* be strong today, because the alternative meant running for the rest of my life.

THE CAB honked its horn, and I sucked in a deep breath. For several moments I stared out my window and kept saying it wouldn't be as bad as I imagined. But no matter what I told myself, I knew it would be.

During the whole trip, I huddled in the backseat, stomach in knots. I wanted—needed—to do this, but in my head, I saw only more problems, regardless of how the conversation went. The cab driver had been less than pleased when he had to drive all the way out to my place, but I'd given my lawyer permission to make it worth his while to chauffeur me around. Obviously it worked, since he'd picked me up.

Getting into the back of this man's vehicle ranked up there with the toughest things I'd ever done. When the door opened and the stale air and sweaty body odor wafted out, I'd had to swallow back the bile that started to rise in my throat.

"Where you headed, kid?" he barked.

My heart hammered. Every instinct told me what I had set out to do would only cause me pain, but I had to try. For myself, as well as Charlie. "The hospital," I replied quietly.

Even though Fall Harbor had less than a thousand people, the town's hospital served the surrounding counties as well, making it a busy place all year round. When the cab pulled up, I got out before he'd even come to a complete stop. Knowing the fare had been paid, I rushed inside, hoping to feel more secure in an enclosed place.

The strong antiseptic smell stung my nose and made me sneeze. I hadn't been to a hospital or doctor's office since I'd moved. Fortunately, eating healthy had apparently been good for me, because other than a few colds and one nasty case of the flu where I still tried to force myself to get up and do my chores—that ended with me not having the strength to get out of bed and collapsing back onto it—I didn't often get sick.

There were so many people bustling around, like little ants, that I wanted to run home. Tension caused my joints to ache, and my stomach knotted so hard it hurt. The only way I could put one foot in front of the other was to keep up a litany in my head that I was doing this for Charlie.

As I followed the signs to the desk, I thought I saw a few people I knew but didn't have the desire to stop and talk to them. I had come for one thing, and once I had it, I'd hop back into the cab waiting to take me home.

"Can I help you?" the perky blond man—Aaron, according to his name tag—behind the counter asked.

"I'm looking for Charlie Carver's room, please," I whispered.

"I'm sorry, what was that name?"

"Carver," I repeated, spelling it out for him.

His fingers flew over the keyboard in front of him. "Okay, let's see. Ah, here we go." Then he frowned. "Are you family?"

"No, I—"

"Then I'm sorry, I can't give you any information on the patient."

I inhaled, then exhaled. This so wasn't helping. "I don't want information. I want to find his room so I can visit with him."

Aaron's eyebrows went up. "Excuse me, *sir*," he said, his voice dripping with condescension, "but we don't allow nonfamily members to visit patients in the ICU."

Intensive Care Unit? But Clay hadn't said that. He told me Charlie would be fine. My breaths started coming faster, harsher. My eyes blurred, and it seemed like the room was spinning. Voices around me were garbled—nothing made sense. I reached for my phone, but couldn't make out any of the buttons because my hands were shaking so hard. When someone grabbed me, I cried out and dropped to the floor, pulling my legs up and wrapping my arms around myself in a vain hope of protection.

Warm hands touched my face, but this time I had no strength to fight back. I'd tried and failed, and it had all fallen apart. I lay on the ground, sobbing, until a voice cut through the buzzing in my head.

"Matt? Matt!"

Someone picked me up and pulled me to their body. Warmth. Safety. I could feel myself being moved. Then, blessed silence. Someone held me, rocked me as they crooned a familiar song. It took me a few moments to recognize "All the Pretty Little Horses." It was a song our mom used to sing to me and Clay when we were kids.

"You with me?"

The voice tugged at me, and I looked up into the gray eyes so very much like my own. "Clay...," I croaked.

He had a watery smile, though I could see the anger in his eyes. "What the fuck did you think you were doing?" he groused. "How the hell did you even get here? You better not have walked, or so help me God, I will kick your ass."

I swallowed hard. My throat hurt and my tongue felt swollen. "Wanted to see Charlie," I whispered. "Didn't know he was in ICU, and they won't let me in."

"In the... who the hell told you that?" he demanded.

"Guy at the desk said only family could get into the ICU. Why didn't you tell me? He's going to die, isn't he?"

"Son of a...." Clay pulled my face so close to his I could smell spearmint on his breath. "Listen to me, Matt. Charlie is most definitely *not* in the ICU. When you calm down, we can go see him together, okay?"

"But he said—"

"He was wrong. I wouldn't lie to you, you know that. Charlie is hurting, but he's not dying."

The tears wouldn't stop. I had visions of Charlie laid out in the morgue, and my heart broke. Clay went back to singing the song, nearly rocking me. It helped me to get my breathing under control.

"How did you get here, Matt?" Clay asked sharply, drawing my attention back to him.

I blinked, then wiped my thumb and forefinger over my eyes. "I took a cab."

"You left your house, got in a cab, and came here just so you could see Charlie?" I nodded, and Clay pulled me in for a bear hug. "I'm so proud of you," he said, kissing my forehead. "I know he's going to be thrilled to find out you're here."

Clay helped me to my feet, then wrapped his arm around my shoulder and held me close as we made our way to the elevators. It took three tries before we found one that didn't have too many people on it. We got in, Clay never loosening his grip, which I appreciated. We walked down the hall, passed by the nurse's station, and entered a room. I found myself equal parts relieved and horrified by the way Charlie looked. His face had bruises that were barely visible under the reddened skin. His leg had a bright blue wrap around it and had been slightly elevated. His hospital gown hung open, his bare chest on display, allowing me to see where he'd hit with enough force to bruise. What hurt the most was seeing his left hand in a cast. I couldn't imagine a writer not having the use of one of his hands.

"He's been asleep for a while. He's been given some meds to help with that," Clay whispered. "I need to file a report about the accident and make a few phone calls. I had been on my way down to get some information when they called about a disturbance. Didn't know it was you. How about if you sit with him while I go take care of this stuff? I'll stop and talk to the nurses and ask them to hold off on coming in here for now. Will that work?"

I nodded, not taking my eyes off Charlie. My lungs ached less, seeing him with my own eyes. Clay directed me to the chair near the bed and helped me to sit down.

"Will you be okay if I'm gone for thirty minutes?"

"Yes," I whispered.

He leaned close, brushing back my hair, and once again laid a kiss on my forehead. "So proud of you, you just don't know."

Any other time the gesture would have annoyed me. In fact, I wouldn't have allowed it. But right now, all I could do was say a silent prayer of thanks that Charlie was okay. I heard the door close, and then we were alone. Words filled my head, but I had no idea what to do with them. They all sounded stupid. Instead I reached out and gently touched his hand. The connection between us soothed my nerves, and my breath finally evened out.

Brown eyes fluttered open and Charlie glanced up at me. "Wow," he whispered. "Must be getting the good drugs."

"Why's that?" I asked.

He gave me a sloppy grin. "For a minute I thought you were really here."

I smiled. Loopy Charlie seemed so different from the man I'd met. But I had to admit, just as adorable. "I am," I answered.

He tried to turn, presumably to get a better look, then winced. I drew my hand back, but he caught it and held it in his. "Don't pull away, Matt. You always pull away. I wish you wouldn't."

Butterflies tickled my belly as he gave a warm smile. "Okay. How do you feel?"

"Like I went over a cliff and hit a tree."

I couldn't help but chuckle. "You did."

"Oh. Well, in that case, I'm doing fine," he said, giving me a goofy smile. "Even better since I know you're really here." He tugged my hand, causing me to lean forward. "Were you afraid when I didn't show up?"

"Yes," I whispered, my voice ragged. I squeezed his hand harder, then let it go. "I didn't like it at all. I tried to call, but you didn't answer."

"I'm sorry. I didn't mean to scare you. I left your place, and as I was headed back down the pass, a rabbit darted out in front of me. I swerved to avoid it, never thinking about the drop-off. I tried to turn away, but gravity is a bitch. As for my phone, I had it in my shirt pocket, so parts of it are probably embedded in my chest. I bought shirts with pockets because I thought they'd be handy for carrying things when I ran. I may need to think it through some more."

I laughed and choked at the same time.

"Come here," he said, raising his arm up a few inches.

There wasn't even any hesitation. I needed proof he was okay, so I moved close. He wrapped his arm around me and gently pulled me into his embrace.

"I don't want to hurt you," I told him.

"Just be gentle," he replied. "Believe me, a hug is good medicine."

It felt good to be held. I'd missed it so much. The discomfort still existed, but I pushed back against it as hard as I could. I wanted this more than I'd wanted anything in a long time. I was unable to hold back the tears, and they started to fall. Charlie rubbed my head while I cried. I tried to step back, but he curled his fingers in my hair and held me in place. My first instinct was to pull away, because this was too reminiscent of what my teacher had done. I couldn't deny my heart was hammering, but it was Charlie, and he was hurt. I took a couple of deep breaths and did my best to keep calm. My need to comfort him overrode my need to break away. Just barely, but I was proud of myself.

"I need the hug," he said. "I was afraid too."

He lay there holding me close to him, my tears soaking his chest. I could hear his raspy breathing, but it told me he was alive and whole.

"You're a very special man, Matt Bowers. I'm glad I got to meet you."

My emotions were all over the grid. Giddy, angry, happy… all of them at the same time.

"What I am is messed up," I admitted. "You don't even want to know how hard it was for me to come here." When I realized what I'd said, I stuttered, hoping to take it back. No need for him to know about my issues right now.

But he kissed my cheek. "I can imagine. And I'm honored you were able to make it."

He didn't tease, didn't condemn. He just let me know my presence was welcome. But if he was going to welcome me, he should know what kind of person I am.

"You should know—"

"I know all I need to," he interjected. "Right now, tell me something that makes you happy."

Taking a moment to gather my thoughts, I tried to stand. This time he let me, but continued to hold my hand. "I read the first three books," I said proudly.

"Get out! You so did not." He grinned, and I was happy I was able to please him.

"I couldn't put them down. They're amazing. You have a true gift." He blushed and his grin morphed into a brilliant smile.

"And I really appreciated your note," I added.

When he yawned, I disentangled our hands and sat next to his bed. "Sorry," he murmured.

"Nothing to it. Go ahead and get some sleep."

"Don't wanna. I'm afraid you won't be here when I wake up."

The door opened and Clay stepped into the room, paper bag in hand. "Well, it's about damn time you woke up," he teased.

"Hey, Sheriff." Charlie yawned again.

"Looks like you're ready for another nap."

Charlie nodded, his head lolling to one side. "Don't let him leave, okay?" he mumbled. "Matt needs to be here when I wake up…." His eyes closed.

"We should let him sleep," Clay said, putting a hand on my shoulder and guiding me toward the door. "I'll take you home."

"But he said I should be here," I protested, trying to look back at Charlie.

"He's been asleep pretty much since they brought him in. He's probably going to sleep through the night. His sister should be here tomorrow, and she'll take care of him."

That had been why I came. Charlie would be leaving, and there wasn't a guarantee he'd come back. The thought of not seeing him every morning upset me in ways I couldn't even describe. He'd come into my life and wedged himself in, nice and tight.

"I don't want him to go," I told Clay, watching Charlie as he slept. He looked so peaceful and innocent. Did I really want to drag him down with my crap?

"I know. I don't either. But he needs someone to help him out. The doctors say he's going to be needing help for six weeks or more, and then there will be physical therapy for his hand and maybe his leg. He's got some things to deal with down the road."

Charlie's words came to me again: *It takes courage to ask for help.*

"I want to help him," I said, my voice far stronger than I expected.

Clay patted my shoulder. "That's nice, but you're not really in a position to help out."

I faced Clay, determined for him to see how serious I was. "I want him to stay with me. I want to be the one to help him."

Clay stepped back and gazed intently at me. "Matt, this isn't something you can just spring on me. You've never wanted anyone in your house. Do you know what help he's going to need?"

"I'll ask," I replied, jutting out my jaw. "I don't want him to go. I need him here. I need him… to stay."

Clay shook his head. "I don't know if this is a good idea."

Now I was pissed. "Why not? You're the one who said I had to get to know him. Well, I did. And I like him."

"I like him too," Clay stressed. "But I'm not able to take care of him. We're not family—we're just friends. You're already under a lot of stress. Look at you down in the lobby. Be honest, can you take care of Charlie? Can you have him in your house for weeks on end? And with winter coming up, what happens if you get snowed in like you did two years ago? You'd be trapped in the house with another person. Do you really think you're able to handle that?"

When he said it like that, I had to pause. I had created a fantasy in my head, one where Charlie would stay with me, in my home, and I'd take care of him. But the reality of the matter had stepped up and slapped me in the face.

"Matt? Do you understand what I'm asking you?"

And until that very moment, I thought I had.

CHAPTER SEVEN

I REFUSED to leave, hoping Charlie would wake up. Clay grudgingly said okay and that he'd look in on me. It turned out he'd been right. Charlie slept soundly for several hours. The nurses checked him routinely, and I sat in the corner of the room, out of the way. Clay had told them to leave me be, and they did, a fact I was grateful for.

When they told us that visiting hours were ending soon, Clay again offered me a ride home. When I told him I had a cab waiting, he said he'd already taken care of that. "You want a ride, you call me. I'd be more comfortable having you with me than someone you don't know."

I didn't argue. If Charlie would be leaving, I wanted a chance to say goodbye, though the thought had me all twisted up inside. My brother hadn't been wrong. I could take care of myself, despite the loneliness I now knew had been buried deep inside me for a long time. But the fact that my fears kept me away from people showed I wouldn't be able to have Charlie in my house, no matter how much I wanted it.

Clay showed up at my place about ten the next morning to take me back to the hospital to see Charlie. It worked, because that would be the time I'd normally see him, so I talked myself into going. Like he'd done the day before, Clay had his arm around me as we walked.

"I talked to Aaron yesterday. He was the young man at the desk. Do you remember him?"

Oh yes, I most certainly did. My stomach still hadn't completely settled. "Oh?"

"He claimed you spoke so softly, and there were so many things going on, he misheard you. He said he's very sorry, and if you want, he'll apologize to you if you come back to the desk today."

The whole confrontation stood out in my mind. I had been so nervous that I hadn't spoken up, even when he questioned what I asked for.

"No. He's probably right," I admitted.

"I thought as much from when I found you."

My stomach roiled. Leave it to Clay to poke at the embarrassment.

"Do you remember me telling you how proud of you I am?" He squeezed my shoulder gently. When I looked at him, the emotion stood out clearly. He wasn't kidding. He really was proud of me.

"Thank you," I muttered.

"I know how hard it is for you, doing things like this. I honestly never thought you'd be able to do it."

I looked down at the linoleum flooring as I clenched my fingers, pressing the nails into my palm to keep me in the moment. "Makes two of us."

"I need to ask, though. Can you tell me why? I mean, for years I've been trying to get you to come to town so you could see me or Mom. But you never did. Yet you got into a cab and came to the hospital to visit Charlie. Why?"

"What can I say that you'll believe? What's the right answer?"

"There isn't one. I'm just curious."

Why could I come to see Charlie when I hadn't really seen much of my family in several years? How was it that Charlie could sit on my porch and sip lemonade? Why did I accept a gift from him when I'd always been self-reliant? The answer seemed very simple, but at the same time, too complicated.

When I looked up, Clay had guided us into the chapel. There wasn't anyone else in the room, and I breathed a sigh of relief.

"I figured this might be an easier place for you to talk."

Years before, I'd gone to church with my family. It had become a tradition from the time when my father was alive. After the incident, I couldn't go anymore. For a long time, I railed against everyone who didn't keep me safe—my mother, the sheriff, our school board, and even God. Eventually I ended up realizing my mother had nothing to do with it and forgave her. Everyone else, not so much.

Walking into the rectory wasn't as uncomfortable as I thought it might be. A small statue of Jesus stood in the middle of the room. Clay walked up and knelt before it, crossing himself as he did. I didn't feel like it was right for me to do it when I couldn't even be sure I still believed. Wanting to show the respect I'd been taught since I was a kid, I did incline my head.

Clay took a seat in one of the short wooden pews and leaned forward, resting his elbows on his knees. "So talk to me."

"What do you want me to say? You know what happened. When we were kids, you saw how it affected me. Charlie is the first person to not make me feel awkward. I don't mean I'm completely comfortable with him, but after all those months of seeing him every day—"

"And calling me to complain about it, of course."

I ignored him. "He became a part of my world. Like my books, or like the animals on my property. He fit there."

He got up and moved over to me. He sat beside me and sighed. "That doesn't make any sense," he told me, the frown on his face punctuating his point.

"But it does to me. Sort of." I tapped my temple. "In here, it makes perfect sense. My world has to be all laid out for me. It's got to have symmetry. When Charlie started running by the house, he stripped that away. It made me edgy and irritable—" Clay raised a hand, and I glared at him until he dropped it again. "But as time went by, and he came every day, same time, same route, I began to accept him there."

"But you kept calling."

For what I had to say, I couldn't look at him. I turned my gaze away and sat in a pew the next row over. "The reason for that is because…." I sighed. "I felt an attraction to him."

For a moment everything was quiet. Though I knew Clay was still beside me, I turned to look at him.

His eyes were wide and his mouth opened and closed a few times. "But you haven't—"

"Not since that day, no. After what Jackson did to me, I couldn't…." I should have been embarrassed saying this to him, but Clay knew me better than pretty much anyone. He nodded knowingly. "I even stopped getting wood in the morning."

"But you got… aroused by Charlie?"

"Just one time," I admitted. "But it happened. And not only that, I also like looking at him. He's big, but I don't feel at all threatened when he's near. In fact, that day you guys came out to the house to fix my door, I realized how safe I felt around both of you. I thought I wouldn't, but when you sat on the swing with me, you seemed to be holding the world at bay."

Clay smiled at me, got up, and moved closer. The nervousness I'd always thought would be there wasn't. At least not like I expected it to be. "I'll always be there for you, Matt. You're not just my brother—you're my best friend. You have been forever. I can't tell you how much it hurt to see you falling apart and not be able to do anything about it."

"I'm sorry," I said, my voice cracking. "I never even thought—"

"No!" he ground out as he pointed his finger at me. "Don't you *ever* apologize. You were a kid, Matt. You never should have had to be concerned with whether a teacher, someone you should have been able to trust, was going to take you out and try to…." He clasped his hands and looked up at the statue of Jesus. His face had gone bright red, and I could see his eyes shine. "It's not fair," he said. "The biggest concern you should have had was a zit or whether Marty Hendricks would find his balls and ask you to go to the school dance."

My gaze snapped up. "How did you—"

He frowned at me and waved his hand. "Please. You mooned over him for more than a year. Mom and I both saw it. For the record, he finally did come out. He moved to California, got married, and he and his husband have a four-year-old daughter."

I chuckled. "Is there anything you don't know?"

Clay sat quietly for a moment. "I don't know how to make it better for you. I never did. You were the reason I went into law enforcement. I wanted to try to help someone the way I wished I could have done for you. I wasn't kidding when I said I wanted my brother back."

He stood and held his arms open. The twinges of anxiety were still there, but I reminded myself that Clay's arms meant safety. I rushed to him and allowed him to hug me.

"I'm trying."

He stepped back, holding my arms, and stared into my eyes. "I can't believe I'm going to say this…. I think you should ask Charlie to stay with you."

He must have seen my shock, because he got a wide grin.

"Yeah, I'm feeling the same way," he said. "But after what you said, maybe Charlie's good for you. You're so much different than you were a few months ago. I know you're still nervous, and it's written all over your face, but you're not manic anymore. You conquered your fears and came here. For him. I have no idea how he feels about you, but maybe it's not a bad idea to find out." He looked down at his wrist. "His sister should be here in about an hour. You have to make up your mind what you want. Then decide if you're willing to go for it."

And that uncertainty had always been my problem.

"I'M SORRY I crashed on you," Charlie said, giving me a small grin. "Didn't know I could be that tired."

He still looked exhausted. The burns on his face had been dotted with a white cream. They didn't seem as bad as they had, which I found myself grateful for. I winced when I saw the hand with the cast. His fingertips had turned black and blue and were still swollen.

"Are you in a lot of pain?"

He smiled at me. "I've got some medication for pain relief. The doctor said I'll need it because of the ribs. When he told me they were broken, I had visions of bone chips floating through my body. He said they're cracked, which is bad enough. Taking a deep breath sucks, but I need to do it on occasion to make sure I don't get pneumonia or something. It could have been a lot worse than it was, so he says. If I had a newer truck, I might not even have gotten burned when the airbag deployed. Of course, that point is moot. Now I'm going to have to get a new one."

"I talked to the paramedics," Clay said. "You have no idea how lucky you were. It took them almost an hour to get to you because where you went down was mostly shale. They had to go very carefully to avoid breaking off chunks that could have done more damage to you and the vehicle. And that tree? You'll be happy to know that it kept you from falling a lot farther down. All in all, you should be grateful, because a few more feet one way or the other and we wouldn't be having this conversation."

Clay had always been blunt, but telling a person they're lucky they didn't die seemed out of character for him. Then I looked in his eyes and saw fear there. He got snappy when he was afraid. I'd been on the receiving end of that often enough. I reached out and touched his arm. He faced me and stepped back.

"I need to get some air," he snarled, then turned and walked away.

"What's wrong with him?"

I shrugged. "You probably scared him."

"Oh, I'm sure I scared myself a lot more. Wouldn't be surprised if I crapped myself on the way down."

"It's not funny," I shouted, then remembered where we were and lowered my voice. "It's not something you should joke about."

"No, it's not," he agreed, holding out his good hand. "But I'm safe, so I have to laugh about it."

I took his hand, and he wrapped his fingers around mine. The same safety I'd felt before blanketed me once more.

"You know, I didn't mean to scare you."

I snorted. "You claimed that yesterday, but that doesn't change the fact that you did."

"Well, then, I'm sorry I worried you. How's that?"

"Better."

His fingers squeezed mine, and warmth rushed through me. I stood looking at our joined hands, marveling at the fact I didn't pull away. In fact, I never wanted him to let go.

"Matt, I—"

"Well," said a voice from behind me, "look who's being lazy."

I tried to draw away, but Charlie held me in place. A woman strolled in, all smiles and attitude. I could tell from the way she favored his good looks that this had to be his sister.

"Teresa!" he said happily. "When did you get here?"

"About fifteen minutes ago. The doctor said you can get out today."

Charlie glanced up at me. "Yeah, that's what I hear."

"So I figure we'll stay overnight at your place while I get you all packed up. Tomorrow we'll get a ride to the airport—though if you have any pull, I really don't want to pay a cab eighty bucks to take us back—and by eight tomorrow night, we'll be home in New York."

"That's... great," he murmured, finally letting my hand slide free of his. "Teresa, this is Matt. Matt, my sister Teresa."

Why I expected her to descend on me, I don't know, but she stood there and graced me with a pearly-white smile. "It's a pleasure to meet you. Charlie's told me about you."

He had? "You did?"

"I did," he confirmed. "Told her what wonderful people lived in Fall Harbor, and how grateful I am that I got to meet so many of them."

Teresa pursed her lips. "Yep. From the waitress at the diner who gives him crappy lemonade, to the man who'd never read one of his books but serves the best lemonade he'd ever had, I constantly get to hear about this town and its colorful residents. I know he's going to miss it here."

I took a small step away from the bed. "But he's coming back. Aren't you?"

He gave me a sad expression and shook his head. "I had a great time here," he said. "But in New York, I can be closer to my publisher, and it'll be easier to go on book tours. Being several hours away from a major airport causes all kinds of problems. I do love the town, but writing is my livelihood."

"Oh, okay," I replied, not knowing what else to say.

He reached for my hand again, and I took another step away, just out of his reach.

"Matt? Can you come back here, please?"

My mouth had gone dry, and with his sister at the door, I felt trapped. "No, I—I should go."

As I edged toward the door, Teresa moved toward me. "Matt? Are you okay?"

I nodded sharply. "Yes, but... I really need to leave."

"Matt, don't—"

In a burst of energy born of desperation to get out of the situation, I darted for the door. When I got into the hall, Charlie called my name, but going back wouldn't do any good. There were too many people, too much noise. I needed my home, where it was safe, where no one would bother me. Where I could once again start building my walls to keep other people out. If nothing else, this had taught me a valuable lesson: Don't pin your hopes on anyone else, because ultimately they'll disappoint you.

ONE GOOD thing about having lived in a small town was knowing there weren't a lot of people on the streets in the afternoon. I'd turned my phone off because Charlie had called four times by the time I hit Main Street—yes, it was really called that. So much had changed in the years since the incident. Many of the shops that had been there almost fifteen years ago were gone, replaced by other things. Mr. Duncan had owned the Creamery, an ice cream parlor that only opened in the summer, but it wasn't there anymore. Instead there was a Dollar Mega Store. Mr. and Mrs. Kwan had owned the dry cleaner shop, but they'd moved out and that building stood vacant, with the windows boarded up. It saddened me to see how much had changed.

I'd just reached the edge of town when the squad car pulled up beside me.

"Get in," Clay ordered.

I did as he said, sliding into the passenger seat and buckling my seat belt.

"Why didn't you wait for me?"

"Didn't know where you were," I replied tersely. "And I needed some air too."

He had the decency to at least appear apologetic. "Sorry about that. When I looked at him, I pictured the accident. I couldn't believe how close he'd come to dying, and it bugged me. After losing Dad, I think I've had enough of car crashes."

Our father had died when his car spun out of control into the path of an oncoming car one winter night. He didn't even make it to the hospital. I'd been eight when it happened, and Clay had been too young to understand anything more than Daddy wasn't coming home again.

"So what happened?"

I sighed and leaned my head against the window. "His sister showed up. Charlie said that he wanted to go back to New York because that's where everything was for him."

Clay pulled the car over to the curb, turned off the engine, and pinned me with a stare. "Is that exactly what he said?"

"He said it was closer and going for book tours would be easier."

"And what did you tell him?"

A shrug of my shoulders was the only answer I could give.

"You didn't say anything, did you?" Clay blew out a breath. "So you're going to let him get on a plane and leave, then go back to your place and hide yourself away for the rest of your life? Is that what you want?"

I turned to glare at Clay. "Yes!" I shouted.

"Why in the hell would you want that?" he demanded.

"Because it's easier than…." I lowered my voice. "Than being hurt again."

Clay dropped back, banging against the headrest. He scrubbed a hand over his face and muttered something under his breath. Then, without looking at me, his voice so soft I could barely hear it, he said, "Life is hurt, Matt. We hurt when Dad died. We hurt when you were assaulted. We hurt when you cut yourself off from your family. We either learn to deal with it or we don't really live anymore."

We sat there as I mulled over his words. Clay made sense, but to my mind, I'd had enough hurt to last me my whole life already and couldn't be sure I had it in me to deal with more.

"Matt?"

"Please take me home," I whispered as the first raindrops began to fall.

Clay stopped talking. He put the car into gear and drove me home. I got out and closed the door and, without looking back, walked inside. I heard him pull away a few minutes later. I took a seat on the couch and stared out the window at the drizzle that threatened to become more as the night wore on. Somewhere along the way, I guess I drifted off.

Thunder cracked overhead, startling me from sleep. The storm had begun in earnest and the rain poured down, drenching everything. The dark weather mirrored my mood. I glanced over at the clock, surprised to see it had gotten to be almost eight already. Everything—from my head to my feet—ached. Despite the discomfort, I walked through the house several times, touching my items, remembering how they'd all come into my life. The books Charlie had given me had me stopping at the shelf they were on. I ran my fingers over them, tempted to take down book four—*Where the Bodies Grow Wild*—and immerse myself in a bit of fiction for a while, but all I could think of was the fact that Charlie had left.

That night when I went to bed—a vow on my lips that tomorrow would be better—sleep took forever to come. Instead I tossed and turned, unable to get comfortable. The storm outside continued to rage, now with high winds adding to the cacophony of the night. The rain pelted the sheet metal roof, sounding like hammer taps. I usually enjoyed storms, but not tonight. All I really wanted was peace and quiet, something I hadn't really had since meeting Charlie. It would be good that he left. It might take me some time to accept it, but once I had, I'd see it was for the best. That thought in my mind, I finally slept.

Nightmares were common for me. Mr. Jackson had given my mind fodder to generate an apparently endless supply of them. Tonight wasn't an exception. Normally everything started in my old car. It went as it always did, me driving with him in the passenger seat, but it quickly became the thing that still haunted me. His hands on me, his mouth. This dream started somewhere new. My property. It had always been a sanctuary to me, a place I would be safe. Not this time. He stalked me through the woods, laughing as I bolted in a panic. No matter how quickly I went, his breath was on my neck. He found my screams funny as I cried out for someone to save me.

Then he was there, grabbing me, pulling me against him. I no longer felt the icy fingers; instead warmth surrounded me, shielding me from everything else.

"He can't hurt you, Matt," a voice whispered close to my ear. "He won't ever be able to hurt you again. I promise."

The noises faded into the background. Mr. Jackson vanished like woodsmoke in a breeze. Everything went silent around me. The only thing that hadn't changed was being held, almost cradled. Tears stung my eyes at the memories of how much I wanted this after what that bastard did to me. Instead I had sat there for hours, asking myself what I'd done wrong. What had I said or done to make him think I wanted that with him? It took years for that chill to finally dissipate, though every now and again a dream would bring it back full force. At this moment, however, someone held me, told me only Mr. Jackson was at fault.

As I sank into the feelings of love and caring, I finally dared to look up. Honestly, in dreams like this, Clay would be the person I'd usually see. He had tried so hard to protect me when he could, even when we were kids. But when deep-set brown eyes met mine and a crooked smile greeted me….

I woke up shivering, and not from the nightmare. My engorged cock stood tall and proud, begging to be touched. Stroked. Fondled. In my mind I could only see Charlie. His face, that grin, the body that captured my attention. Tentatively I reached down to rub my erection, fully expecting it to wither as it did the last time. When I slid my fingers along the smooth skin, much to my surprise, it got harder.

After spitting into my palm, I wrapped my hand around my dick, relishing the feel that had been denied me for too many years. Long, smooth strokes up and down had me moaning, thrusting up into my hand, and all the while Charlie was on my mind. In my imagination he caressed me reverently, his touch so light as to almost not be there, but I knew it was. He pressed his lips against my neck, nibbling on the skin, bringing up goose bumps, whispering to me how much he wanted to be inside me, how much he needed to taste me.

He'd be on his knees and lower his face to my crotch to lap at my balls, then up my shaft until his tongue swirled around the head, and then he'd bob up and down as he worked to take me all the way to the base. He would press his fingers against my pucker, and I'd spread my legs for him, allow him to touch where no one else had ever gotten close.

"Matt," he'd whisper, his voice husky.

I orgasmed so hard it splattered on the headboard and seemed like there would be no end to it. My body rocked from the sensations, and I cried out Charlie's name as all the pent-up emotions rolled through me. When it finally subsided, I could feel the cooling liquid sliding down my stomach and onto the bed.

The overwhelming sense of relief brought tears of joy to my eyes. I'd had my first orgasm in thirteen years. Then reality hit me square in the face: the person who'd been responsible for it had left and gone to New York to start his life over again.

And I'd let him go.

CHAPTER EIGHT

WHEN MORNING broke, I had no desire to get out of bed. The dried residue on my stomach reminded me that last night I'd had an orgasm. A knock-down, drag-out, oh my God, what the fuck orgasm. It had been the highlight of my night, obviously. But now sunshine peeked into my windows, and I needed to get up and move. So much to do today. There were wild brook trout to catch that would stock one of my freezers for the upcoming winter, seeds to be collected so that next year I could have sunflowers again, canning to do so the vegetables I harvested would help feed me through the long winter ahead. And a man I never got the chance to talk to would need me to start missing him now, because he'd be in New York soon.

A quick shower and a round of touching the items in my house, because I needed the grounding, and maybe there was a chance I could face the day. The air was cool, and a foggy mist had settled over the area. Chances were good that it would burn off by late morning, but there had been days it stuck around because of the higher elevation. Today needed to not be one of those. I had to keep busy, occupy my mind as much as possible. Any distraction would give me time to think, and I definitely didn't need that.

The stream would be my first destination. Having it on the property was one of the reasons this plot of land suited my needs perfectly. Fed by the lake in Ash Hills, there would be smallmouth bass, brook trout, and whitefish at various times throughout the year, and my love of fish made it ideal for me. After collecting my equipment, I hiked down to the closest point and spent the next ninety minutes doing my best to bring home some good eats.

Making my way back to the house with a stringer that held eight fish, I stupidly checked my watch. It said 9:46 a.m., and that caused an ache in my chest, because today at ten, there would be no Charlie. No greeting from over the fence or requests for lemonade. Today would be peaceful and quiet, the way it always had been. I swallowed down the lump in my throat, wondering why that didn't hold the appeal it always had.

After entering the house, I stored the fish in the refrigerator to be dealt with as the sun started to set. That would allow me to work in the yard while enough light let me see clearly.

The sunflowers were my next stop. I gathered all the seeds I could, separating them into three piles. One pile would be used to plant next year, one would be roasted, because they were delicious, and the last—and largest—pile would be used for my birds to help them survive, should the winter turn exceptionally harsh. As the last flower came down and I shucked the seeds, I heard a strange noise from down the road. To my ears it almost sounded as though someone was… grunting. I stood a few more moments, until I saw a sight that had me almost crying.

"Your lemonade fresh?" Charlie asked, his voice pitched low enough that it sent shivers up my spine.

Teresa stood behind the wheelchair, pushing for all she was worth. Her face was beet red, her breathing labored. But the only thing I truly saw was Charlie. He quirked an eyebrow at me, and I sputtered to answer.

"Yes. Well, no. I mean, I made some the day you… that day. But I have a pitcher."

Teresa stopped outside my gate. "I could really go for a glass," she panted. "This bastard is heavy."

Charlie turned and looked at her. "Why don't you go back to your truck? I'll call you when we're done here."

She stood, hands on her hips, and glared at him. "You're kidding," she huffed. "I just pushed you up a freaking hill the size of Everest. Don't I get to catch my breath first?"

"Teresa," Charlie said softly.

"No, I—she can…," I stuttered.

"She'll be okay, Matt." He looked up at Teresa. "Please."

She snorted. "Fine." Then she turned on her heel and stormed away.

"May I come in?" Charlie asked.

I rushed to the gate and pulled it open for him. He wheeled himself in, though rather unsteadily. "Your sister is upset," I mentioned.

68

"She'll get over it," he insisted, rolling up to the stairs on the porch. "I'm more concerned about you."

He sounded unhappy. When I got to where he sat and saw his crinkled brow and stormy eyes, there could be no doubt. He was livid. Before I could say anything, he pointed his finger at me. His hands were shaking, and he narrowed his gaze.

"What the hell is wrong with you?" he demanded. "You come to my hospital room, hug me, and then you bolt without even telling me why."

His skin had gone nearly purple in his rage, and I took a few steps back, suddenly grateful for the fact that he had come in a wheelchair and the stairs were nearby.

"Matt," he snarled. "I asked you a question."

"You were leaving," I answered, my voice trembling. "I didn't see the point in waiting."

"No, that's not it." He leaned forward and pinned me with a glare like I'd never seen before. He studied my face; then, when it seemed he'd gotten the answer he wanted, he sat back again.

It struck me at that moment. He wasn't angry. He'd been afraid.

"I saw your face before you left. You were terrified. Do you know how that made me feel? You ran out, and my sister and two nurses had to hold me down to keep me from following you. I demanded she go and bring you back, because I needed to know why you were upset. She said you got on the elevator and she couldn't catch you."

He was still afraid. He gripped the chair, his knuckles white. His body shook, and his eyes were wet with unshed tears. What I had thought to be anger hadn't been that at all. He was worried about me.

"I tried calling, but you wouldn't answer." His breath was coming heavy now. "When I talked to Clay, he said he'd dropped you off at home, so at least I knew you were safe. You have no idea what thoughts were going through my head."

"I'm sorry," I murmured.

"Why did you leave?" he asked, his voice breaking.

Needing to put more distance between us, I backed up onto the first step.

"This is why Teresa needed to bring me. I knew if you saw us coming, you'd hide." Now the hurt in his voice came through loud and clear. "It's what you do, isn't it? Run when you're afraid?"

"You don't know a goddamn thing about me!" I shouted. "You should just go ahead and go back to New York, like you were planning. It's not like you...." I stopped, knowing what the next words out of my mouth were about to be, knowing they could never be taken back.

"Go on. Not like I what? Don't hold back. Finish what you were going to say," he challenged.

To say I withered under his onslaught was an understatement. I glanced nervously at the door behind me.

"Planning to run again? Not like it would be the first time, is it?"

Okay, *now* he'd moved into the angry territory. He rolled a little closer but never stopped staring. "Why do you run, Matt? Just tell me that. Am I that scary? Are you afraid of me? Have I done something to you? What is it? If you want me to leave, at least tell me why. I know something's wrong. It's why I asked Teresa to go. I don't want to see that look on your face, the one where you're going to bolt."

The moment of truth had arrived. I fixed my gaze on a point beyond him, looking instead at the tall trees that dotted the landscape.

"I don't want you to go," I whispered. "That's why I came to the hospital. I wanted you to stay. With me, I mean. I wanted to take care of you until you were better because...." I swallowed. "Because I like you, and I knew that if you left, I would never see you again."

He gave me a sad smile. "Was that so hard? I never wanted to go, but it didn't seem like there was much here for me. And the thing I wanted most didn't seem to be all that into me. For the record, I like you too. Why do you think I continue to jog up here? Or why I brought you the books? They were my excuses to come and see you."

He liked me? My heart danced the Cha-Cha Slide, thumping and jumping. Closing the distance between us, I stood and looked down at him. He reached out with his right hand and wrapped my fingers in his, giving them a light squeeze.

"You're a hard man to get through to. I thought I dropped enough subtle hints, but when they didn't work, I went for a few not-so-subtle ones, but you just didn't seem to get it. So I thought maybe I misread the signs and you weren't into me at all."

I peered down at our joined hands.

"Why are you crying?" he asked.

To be honest, I hadn't known I was. "Not sure. Because you're here? You were supposed to leave."

"Do you really think I could have left without seeing you?"

I gave a shoulder shrug. "You don't know me, so why should you stay?"

"I don't…. Really? Is that what you think? Your name is Matt Bowers. Your brother is the sheriff, though I get the feeling you don't see much of each other. You like detective novels that were written by a very cool author. Those gray eyes twinkle like gems, and you have the rarest, most beautiful smile I think I've ever seen."

I cocked my head. "What do you mean rarest?"

He grinned at me, and I realized he still hadn't let go of my hand. "You don't smile often, so when you do, it's a rare gift. Whoever gets it is very lucky."

Butterfly wings tickled my insides, and my cheeks heated.

"Yes, that smile," he teased. "It's like the Mona Lisa. Impish, yet sweet."

"Stop," I scolded him, as embarrassment caused my cheeks to burn.

"You know you like it. It's written all over your face."

He couldn't know how much I liked it. No one had ever complimented me like this, and without a frame of reference, I had no idea how to handle it.

"So…. Were you serious about me staying with you until I'm healed up?"

He had a hopeful expression, and I couldn't come up with a reason to say no. Not that I wanted to. "Yes, please."

"Okay. I'd like that. I know it's short notice, so is there anything you need?"

"What about your sister?"

He waggled his brows. "You need my sister?"

I stepped back, horrified at what he'd taken my comment to mean. "What? No!"

It took me several moments to catch on to his joke. Charlie's laugh was rich and sent an electric current through my body.

"No, there isn't anything. I have plenty of food."

"Tell me you have lemons?" he pleaded.

"Charlie, would you like a glass of lemonade?" I offered.

"Yes, please. I thought about it all day yesterday. My mouth is puckering already."

The idea of his mouth puckering had me wondering what it would be like to kiss him, to meld our mouths together. I'd heard guys in gym talking about sex, about kissing girls, and I'd always wanted to kiss someone. Not like Mr. Jackson had done. I didn't want to count that as my first kiss. It should be from someone who looked at me the way Charlie was at that moment. It was almost enough to make me believe that maybe I was special.

I bent down, wrapped an arm around him, and helped him to his feet. Once I had him steady, the next trick was getting him up the stairs. Now I understood why Teresa had been straining, because he wasn't light. After I wrangled him into a spot where he'd be out of the sun, I leaned against the pole, wanting a moment to catch my breath. But when Charlie called my name, I looked over and was lost in his gaze.

"Matt?" he said softly, his eyes warm and gentle.

"Y-yes?" I stuttered.

He gave me a lopsided grin. "My lemonade?"

I HELPED him onto the porch and put him into the seat of the swing. He snuggled in, being careful because of his ribs. I grabbed the wheelchair and pulled it onto the porch where he could reach it. Afterward, he made himself at home while I poured him a glass of lemonade and brought it back outside.

"I suppose I should call Teresa and let her know." He chuckled, and I couldn't help but grin. "I can imagine what her reaction will be."

As he dialed, I went into the house to make sure the sheets on the bed were clean. Fortunately the sofa in the living room was relatively lump-free. As I gazed around the room, a jolt of panic struck me. The dark wood bookcases, the small medium-brown stands that held my most prize possessions, my desk, which sat empty, and the painting I'd done in art when I was a freshman of an orange-and-red sunrise as it crested over the crystal blue waters that hung on the wall—this was my world, the one I'd cobbled together. Could I let Charlie stay here? He would be touching my things, making a mess. How the hell could I deal with that?

"I said I'd buy you a ticket home. You can stay in my place for a few weeks and call it a vacation. You'll love the town." Charlie sighed. "Teresa, listen to me." A pause. "No, that's not it at all! I just—"

Another longer pause, then an even deeper sigh. This time I went to the window where I could see him. He glanced up, noticed me, and made a *blah-blah-blah* gesture with his hand.

"Yes, I know you're upset, but I told you, Matt—Oh my God, woman! Will you shut up and let me talk?" He chuckled. "Thank you. I know it's not in your nature to let someone get a word in edgewise." He laughed. "Yes, and the horse I rode in on, I know, I know."

He listened intently for a bit, his eyes displaying deep laugh lines as he listened to whatever Teresa was saying. Everything about Charlie was beautiful. He glanced up and noticed I hadn't moved. He smiled and gave me a wink. That simple gesture had my heart fluttering.

"The hospital shouldn't have called you," he insisted. "I appreciate you coming all this way, but you really didn't need to." He paused. "I should have updated that information a long time ago." He dropped his head back, then shook it from side to side. "I would have been fine, really. They didn't need to get in touch with you. This is where I want to be. I have friends here, and they would have helped me. And before you ask, no, it's got nothing to do with Mitch. If he's happy, then I'll be glad for him, but it's been over for years."

He laughed, and I realized I'd been eavesdropping. Everything in me rebelled against the idea of him staying with me, but this time I pushed back. Charlie could stay here; we could work it out. I had no doubt about that. I stepped out onto the porch and waited while he continued talking to Teresa. It was obvious he loved her, but also that she was able to get under his skin.

"No, you can't come up here for lemonade. Matt and I have a lot to discuss. If you could go back to my place and pack me some clothes, laptop, and other essentials, I would be eternally grateful." He paused. "Matt? Is it okay if Teresa drops a bag off for me? She can leave it on the porch."

"Yes, but she doesn't have to—"

"It's fine, honest." He went back to talking with Teresa. "I'll give you a call in a few days if anything changes. Uh-huh. Yeah, love you too."

He hung up and turned his head in my direction. "Be glad you only have a brother. Sisters are… a challenge at times. Or maybe it's just mine." He laughed. "Either way, if you still want me here, I'd like to stay. If you think it would cause too many problems, I'll have Teresa come get me."

"After that call, she's probably halfway back to New York by now."

"That would be great," he admitted. His smile faded a little. "After the accident, the hospital called her as my emergency contact. She's the one who decided to jump on a plane to come and get me. It's her feeling that I was much happier in New York, and that if I came back, me and my ex could work out our problems. I told her before I didn't want to work it out. The more time I spent away from him, the more I realized we weren't meant for each other. I was in love with love, nothing more."

He held out his hand to me, and without questioning it, I went to him and took it. What surprised me was how natural it seemed that I let him touch me. Until I met Charlie, I never, ever allowed anyone to put their hands on me. Now I found comfort in allowing Clay to hold me when the pressures got to be too much, and Charlie's hands on me felt right.

"Okay, last chance. If you'd rather I not stay here, it's perfectly okay. I know you value your privacy, and I don't want to intrude on that. If you want me to go, I'll stay in town. Teresa will stay and take care of me, I'm sure. There will be a lot of complaining, though. You'll probably be able to hear it way up here. But I want to stay, if you want me to."

There could be no doubt that he was offering me a chance to say no, to say I had made a mistake. The urge to accept it could have easily overwhelmed me, but I swallowed it down. If I ever wanted to have a chance at a normal life, or at least some semblance of one, I had to work hard to show that I could *be* normal.

"Yes, I want you to stay with me. I have the bed made up for you, and...."

Charlie waited patiently while I got my thoughts together. Now that this had become real, I didn't know where to start.

"Is there anything you don't eat?"

He patted his flat stomach. "My mom likes to say I could be a human garbage disposal. Anything and everything."

That would make my life a lot easier. Having limited supplies on hand, I'd have to improvise some meals until the store could make a delivery. Of course, that would mean getting an order in and having Charlie see my routine. Was I really ready for that?

"Charlie?"

"Hmm?"

Not able to look at him, I turned away and began to pace. I couldn't decide if I should sit down or run away. My cheeks were already red-hot. "There won't be a good time to discuss this, and it probably should be said before you decide this is the place you want to be."

He turned and leveled his gaze at me. "Okay. Tell me what's on your mind."

I figured this would be easier if I was sitting, so I took a seat and looked out at the copse of trees that had been almost stripped bare. Funny how this conversation made me feel the same way. "Thirteen years ago...." I paused and tried to come up with a better way to say it, but nothing came to me beyond the bald truth. "Thirteen years ago," I repeated, "a teacher tried to... to...." My throat seized up, and the words wouldn't come.

"Matt? Are you okay?" Charlie reached over and put his hand atop mine. "Tried to what?"

I swallowed hard, and it hurt all the way down. A quick breath, followed by my confession. "He tried to rape me," I whispered.

CHAPTER NINE

THE SILENCE became oppressive. I prayed he heard me, because if he hadn't, there would be no way to repeat what I'd said. He just sat there, but neither of us said anything. Eventually it got to be too much, and I stood, the need to get away riding me hard.

"Where are you going, Matt?" he asked, his voice husky. "Look at me, okay?"

"I have to… I need… I don't know," I cried, scrubbing my hands over my face.

"Look at me," he insisted.

At that moment the truth had become even harder to face, because someone I cared for, a person I wanted to care for me, had heard what happened. Would he understand? Would he reject me? I turned my head slowly, expecting to see disgust or censure in his expression. Instead, what I found was a man with tears in his eyes.

"The only thing keeping me from holding you right now is my leg," he said, a strange tone in his voice that I hadn't heard before. "Can you maybe sit next to me?"

He held a hand out and looked beseechingly at me.

"Please, Matt?"

I took a few tentative steps toward him.

He reached for my hand and pulled me closer. "Why are you telling me now?"

"Because you might decide you don't want to be here," I replied softly, squeezing his fingers.

"No, that's not going to do it," he assured me. "I knew there was something, but it's your story, so you had to talk about it in your own time. I'd never press you to tell me something until you were ready."

His understanding threw me for a loop. Part of the reason I hid out was because I'd already seen the looks of pity on my mother's face and couldn't handle it. If Charlie's expression had been similar, I probably would have fallen apart again. But it wasn't there. Only concern.

Taking a seat next to him, I exhaled slowly. "I was sixteen when it happened. He asked me to give him a ride home, and I didn't think anything of it. He creeped me out, but he was a teacher, right? Trustworthy, supposed to have your best interests at heart. He directed me to drive to a spot outside of town. When we got there, he pawed me, tried to force me to suck him."

As I remembered the incident, my heart thudded so loud Charlie must have been able to hear it. My stomach threatened to revolt at the memories. I swallowed down the bile and continued.

"I threw up on him. He yanked me out of the car and pushed me onto the ground, then kicked me for good measure before he stole my car and drove away. I dragged myself over to a tree and leaned against it, crying over the incident and also wondering what I'd done to cause it. My mom found me hours later after she saw him driving my car through town. They made him tell them where he left me. After that, I kinda fell apart."

Insistent fingers slid through my hair, kneading my scalp. "You're so damn strong," he said.

The laugh that burst from me had nothing to do with humor and everything to do with relief at finally telling my story.

"If you don't want to stay here, I'll understand."

He grunted as he shifted his weight next to me. When his arm went around my shoulder and he pulled me closer, I tensed. "It's okay," he murmured. "I won't hurt you. If this bothers you, tell me and I'll stop."

I didn't say anything, and he urged me to put my head on his shoulder.

"If anyone should expect to be uncomfortable, you'd be the one," he said. "Sharing something like this has to dredge up all kinds of uncomfortable feelings."

Now came the time to bare my soul. "You don't understand. The incident left me with… issues."

He gave a half snort, half chuckle. "If you had said you were fine, I would know you were lying. No one, no matter how strong, would be unaffected by something like that. The physical assault left you open to emotional pain too. Anyone would have, as you say, *issues*."

He didn't even ask to hear what my problems were, but it honestly sounded like he believed in me. My mother—and to an extent, Clay—had always pitied me or expected me to just "get over it." Charlie didn't. It made me feel closer to Charlie than to my own family.

"My therapist says the assault might have opened the door for me to develop OCD and some PTSD."

"What do you think?"

I thought about it for a few moments. The terrors. The need to touch everything to ensure my world was right. The fear of being among people I don't know. "He's not wrong," I admitted. "As long as I'm here, I'm safe. I can't function outside the house."

"But you came to the hospital to see me," Charlie reminded me. He continued to tousle my hair, and his touch grounded me in the moment.

"You don't know what that took," I replied. "There were so many people, and then, when the guy at the desk told me you were in the ICU, I fell apart in the lobby."

He sat back and stared into my eyes. "He told you I was in intensive care?"

I nodded. "Clay said the receptionist misheard me when I asked for your room. He probably did too. I could barely get the words out, and he was busy."

"Aw, Matt. I'm sorry. If my phone hadn't gotten broken, I swear I would have called. Teresa picked up a replacement for me on her way to town. Otherwise I still wouldn't have one."

We sat in silence for a time, and it wasn't at all uncomfortable. A glance at my watch told me we'd been on the porch for nearly three hours, and I didn't want to have him stop touching me. But there were chores that needed to be done, so I pulled away. He squinted at me, then asked, "Everything okay? I didn't do something wrong, did I?"

"No, you were amazing. I mean…. No, you didn't do anything. I have things I have to get done, and I'm behind schedule. I know it's weird, but—"

"It's not. It's part of you, and I think both of us will have to accept it." He gave me a smile, which softened the words. "Is it okay if I stay here?"

"What? Yes, of course. I already said that. Why? Don't you want to stay?" I asked, my voice rising in pitch.

"I meant here on the swing," he said, relaxing into the cushion. "I'm about due for a pain pill and could use a nap. As for leaving, if you want me to go, you're going to have to ask me. And so you know, if you do, I will go without any hesitation."

As much as it shamed me, it settled my stomach, knowing I had options. I had no intention of exercising them, because having Charlie here calmed me. His face, his smile, even his scent settled a lot of the fear that roiled inside.

"Yes, rest." I held up a finger when he started to speak, and then I went into the house, grabbed the blanket from the bed, took it back out, and spread it over him.

"I'm not an invalid," he groused.

"You are for a time," I countered, being gentle as I tucked the blanket under his legs. It felt right, and my stomach flipped at the realization that I was about to have someone in my home and I welcomed him there.

"Matt?"

I glanced up, and he smiled at me. "Yes?"

"Thank you." He picked up his near-empty glass of lemonade and tipped it in my direction. "For everything."

As CHARLIE dozed, I set about canning the vegetables. Potatoes, beans, carrots, tomatoes, and corn. In a few weeks, I would also get a large delivery from the store. Unless the weather stayed mild, this would have to get me—us—through the winter months. And now that Charlie would be here, I needed to order more. I dialed the store and waited.

Six rings later a familiar voice came on the line. "Matt! I wasn't expecting to hear from you."

"Good afternoon, Mr. Gianetti. I wasn't sure you'd answer."

"I'll always answer for you, you know that. I know you don't like talking to other people, and you know you're one of my favorite customers."

Mr. Gianetti had owned a small store with his wife when I was a kid. I would go in and buy a dollar's worth of candy and walk away with a bag big enough for me to share with Clay. Even though I rarely did. I continued going there every day until the incident. After I hit puberty, I went in so I could stare at Milo, one of Mr. Gianetti's sons, as his muscles strained while he worked. With his dark hair and blue eyes, he was a walking wet dream. One day I must have been watching him too intently because Mr. Gianetti caught me. I was worried he'd kick me out of his store or something. Never happened. He simply patted me on the shoulder and smiled, assuring me everything was okay.

"You love who you love, Matty. There's nothing wrong with any of it. Though I think Milo might be a little old for you."

That was it. He said nothing else on the subject.

Clay told me that after I'd moved away, Mr. Gianetti had grown his store into an actual grocery. When I moved into my house, I started doing my shopping over the phone with him, and when I would need something, he would always take my call, never letting anyone else talk to me. I appreciated the stability of our transactions.

"I know this is going to be a little weird, but I need to place another order."

He didn't say anything for a moment. "Was something wrong with what we sent you? If something didn't come out right, you tell me, and we'll make sure to fix it."

"No, everything came perfectly, as always." My stomach tightened. "I've got someone staying with me for a while, and I'm going to need extra things."

"Oh, that's good," Mr. Gianetti said. "I worry about you, out there alone. The missus says you need someone. Is he a good man? Does he treat you right? If he doesn't, you tell me. The boys will have a word with him."

Mr. Gianetti always made me laugh. He always talked to me with a bad, overemphasized accent, like he was a mafia don or something. When I was a kid, he'd do it and waggle his bushy gray eyebrows.

80

"No, he's a good man," I promised. "So no need to rile the boys right now. Maybe later."

His chuckle was warm and brought back good memories. "What do you need, Matty?"

"I think I'm going to need to reorder what I got last time." I fretted, because I didn't know how much Charlie ate and wasn't sure if I'd have enough. "Maybe I should double it."

Mr. Gianetti clucked his tongue. "You'll never go through that much food in three months," he told me. "Best to keep your order light and reorder if you need more."

That idea wouldn't work. It took me long enough to deal with getting new things in the house. Plus, if the weather did turn bad, the likelihood of someone reaching us dropped drastically. "I think I need to, sir. If we get snowstorms, it might not be possible to deliver here."

"We have snowmobiles. I promise, one way or another, we'd get to you, Matty."

And he probably would. The man would move heaven and earth to do something for his customers, including procuring special items for me. It's how he kept growing his business in such a small town. Like the hospital, people came from the surrounding counties because of Mr. Gianetti's willingness to help them. In the town, Mr. Gianetti was the closest thing they had to a true rock star. But the thought of someone coming up this way reminded me of the man sitting on my porch and the accident he'd had.

"I appreciate it, sir, but I think I'd be more comfortable knowing I had it on hand."

Mr. Gianetti sighed. "Okay, if that's how you want to handle it. I hope you have enough space for everything."

Space was one thing I had plenty of. My pantry was huge and would barely be half full after the canning I was doing. There were two large chest freezers where my fish and any other game I took got stored. The house would have been large enough to house a family of three easily, so there was plenty of room.

"I do," I assured him. "I know this is short notice, so if it takes longer to—"

"The order will be there in two weeks, just like I promised. Sometimes you need to have a little faith, Matty."

That was something normally in short supply around here. "I'll try, sir."

"Now, is there anything else you need?"

"Um… not that I can think of."

"What about… you know, protection?"

I laughed. "My brother is sheriff. I think I should be okay on that front."

Mr. Gianetti coughed. "I meant more… personal protection. Something to keep you safe in case…."

Oh. Shit. "Oh, God no." I could feel fire rising in my face at the thought.

"You have to be safe, Matty. You're my favorite customer. I need you around."

"There won't be any of… that," I assured him.

He made a *hmm* sound, then said, "I'll pack it. If you use it, you can thank me later."

I just knew those wild eyebrows of his were waggling.

AFTER I finished with Mr. Gianetti, I canned my first batch of vegetables. Because of the lateness of the day, I decided I would have to wait until tomorrow before I could continue. This threw off my schedule, and the thought had my chest heaving. I tried to calm myself, but there had been too many new things for me to deal with today. I went around the house and did my basic routine, and that relaxed me some, but not as much as it normally would.

I went out on the porch and found Charlie with his head thrown back, mouth wide open. He looked… oh, hell. Adorable was the only word I could come up with. He was snuggled beneath the blanket, clutching it to his chin. I found it strange that seeing him lying out on the porch calmed me more than the routine I'd just put myself through.

I went back inside to start dinner. Tonight would be fresh fish, dredged in flour and spices, then fried nice and crispy and served with fried potatoes and onions from the garden. I loved living up here, away from everyone else. Dependent on myself, mostly eating what I caught or grew. But having Charlie here had me thinking that if I lived closer to town, we could have seen each other more. Maybe we could have gone to the cafe, had a nice dinner. Spent some time together to get to know each other.

"Something smells delicious."

His voice surprised me. I turned and splashed grease on my hand. I cried out, more from shock than anything else.

Charlie yanked the door open and did his best to wheel himself inside. He made a beeline for me and clasped my hand, staring at it intently. "Stick your hand under the cold water," he instructed.

I did as he said. It sent prickles along my arm, but eventually the throbbing stopped, which I found myself grateful for. But what really astonished me was that he hadn't turned my hand loose. While I had it under the water, he held my forearm, moving my hand gently, ensuring that all the red spots were covered.

"I'm so sorry," he murmured, taking my hand and drying it with the dish towel he'd pulled from the counter.

"It's not your fault," I assured him. "I'm not used to people being there, so when you spoke, I got a little startled."

He squinted at me, his brown eyes showing so much concern it made me slightly uncomfortable. "Matt, I—"

The timer for the fish dinged, and we both jumped. I pulled away from Charlie, rushed back to the stove, and turned the burner off. My heart thumped hard as I remembered the expression on his face, the touch of his hand. Tender. Caring. I wanted to know what he was going to say, but the thought of him actually finishing the sentence scared me so much my hands were shaking.

"Dinner should be done in a minute," I informed him, not yet able to turn around. "If you want to wash up, the bathroom is down the hall on the left. There are clean towels in the cabinet, but…. Could you make sure you hang it over the faucet when you're done?"

"Yeah, okay." His voice told me everything wasn't okay, but that he wouldn't push me on it.

He wheeled himself slowly down the corridor. I let my head drop against the cabinet door with a *thunk*. So many emotions, so many thoughts of what could go wrong, and me chastising myself for my decisions. I had to keep in mind this was what I wanted, because right now, I wasn't sure I'd be able to survive having him in the house and not fantasizing about him.

"Matt?" he called out from the bathroom.

I turned toward his voice. "Yeah?"

"Just so you know, this conversation isn't over."

I smiled to myself, even as I banged my head against the cabinet again, because of course he wasn't going to let it go. And a little sliver of hope inside me was grateful, because I honestly hoped he wouldn't.

CHAPTER TEN

THE WEATHER turned decidedly colder not long after I flipped the calendar to November. Frost had hit the plants hard, causing them to shrivel, and the things that hadn't been ripe enough to harvest had fallen off the vines.

"Goddamn, is it always this cold up here?"

Charlie huddled beneath a thick down comforter that I'd pulled from storage and put on the bed. Now that the house had gotten so much chillier, it was time to use both the wood-burning stove and fireplace to throw a little heat. The fireplace was sufficient to heat the living room so I normally used that, but the stove had pipes to take heat to the whole house. I had more than enough wood to keep them going all winter long, so I wasn't worried about that. What did concern me was the fact that the weather didn't normally dip into the single digits for several weeks yet. This didn't bode well for the upcoming winter.

"Not usually so early, but yeah. Colder than a witch's tit, as the saying goes."

"No way can I type when my fingers are numb," he whined.

"Baby."

The teasing had come so easily. The two of us fit together naturally, despite my... idiosyncrasies. Yes, there were challenges. The first one had to do with seeing him naked. Oh my God. Having seen his body when he ran, I knew he was built very nicely, but nude? My mouth watered every time I helped him get clean. I'd wash areas he couldn't reach because of his ribs, and being that close to him, seeing him in that way? I couldn't deny it affected me. Charlie looked completely edible.

The other issues were more problematic, though:

"Charlie? Did you take down *Murder in Times Squared*?"

"Yeah, but I put it back."

But he hadn't. Not really. He'd put it on the shelf, but out of order. My hands itched to put it back, but I needed him to understand what the problem was.

"Could you come here for a minute?"

He got up from the desk, where he was looking at something on the computer. "What's up?"

I bit my lip because I was about to come across as a complete jerk. "Everything has a place." I held out the book. "This is number two in the series, but you put it in the third place."

I'd expected him to sigh or huff or just be annoyed. Instead he took the book from my hands. "I am very sorry," he said, no trace of sarcasm. He put the book back up on the shelf, where it should have been. "Is that better?" he asked.

I reached up and straightened it out, making sure it was in line with everything else. "Thank you. I'm sorry."

"Hey, stop that!" he said sharply. "I'm a guest in your home. You have every right to ask me to help out. Thank you for letting me know."

A few days later, I opened the refrigerator to start lunch and found a gallon of milk with the label facing away. I reached in and pulled it out, then turned it. I wasn't going to say anything, because after the whole book thing, I didn't want him to think I was going to do nothing but complain.

"What are you doing?" he asked from behind me.

I thought about lying but didn't. "The milk was in the wrong way," I said, doing my best to appear nonchalant. "It's fine. I fixed it."

He hobbled over and looked inside. "Well, damn, I guess I did. This is kinda new for me, and I swear I'm trying to learn. I don't want to make your life difficult."

After that, Charlie did his very best to work with me. He watched what I did, then tried to emulate it. I now found him making certain he'd cleaned his plate, dried it, then put it away. Admittedly, I needed to check it myself after he finished, but the fact that he was willing to put himself out there like that went a long way to making our time together much easier.

"Matt? Are you even listening to me?"

His voice pulled me out of my reverie with his petulant tone. He sat there shivering and looking absolutely miserable. "Sorry, what were you saying?"

"Seriously, Matt. I have a deadline, and I've already asked for an extension. My publisher didn't believe I had broken my hand. I had to text her a picture of the cast. She gave me three weeks, because I already missed the first date she gave me."

"But the cast doesn't come off before that," I protested.

He shrugged. "I'll just have to muddle through, I guess. Maybe I'll tell her a block of ice developed around my hand."

I shook my head. Usually throwing on a sweater would keep me warm. "I'll get a fire going. It'll be nice and toasty soon."

I tossed a few logs into the hearth, and it only took a short time before the house was awash in light from a crackling fire. The warm glow it cast about the room was one of my favorite things about winter. Having Charlie to share this simple pleasure with? I sighed. I couldn't believe it when I realized how much I would miss him when he went back to his place.

"Please tell me Teresa packed my long underwear."

Teresa had, very grudgingly, sent a couple of boxes with some clothes, his books, a laptop computer, and a pair of crutches to use in the house. It took me some time to work them into the household, but I knew how important it was for him to have some of his own things here.

Fortunately he was able to get a signal on his phone, and he used it as what he called a tether to communicate with the outside world.

"How do you live without the Internet?" he'd asked one night over hearty vegetable soup and thick, crusty dinner bread dripping with butter.

"What do I need it for?" I countered, standing by the sink and rinsing out my bowl. "It's a distraction I can't afford. It would take time away from my...." I stopped talking because I realized I had said too much.

Charlie put his spoon down and reached for a roll. He slathered butter on it, dipped it in his soup, took a bite, then said, "From your schedule. I understand. I guess I never really thought of it that way. Without the net, I can't check on my books or promote them. Hell, without the net opening the doors for me to discover writing, I wouldn't even be an author."

I cocked my head and thought about how much the world would miss out if Charlie's voice was silenced. His writing was phenomenal and showed that gay characters weren't caricatures or something to be used as a running gag. They were forceful, powerful, and always in control. Even when Tremaine let Lucien take care of him, he still retained his "fuck the world" attitude. They gave me hope, and to think they could be nothing but an idea in a young man's head because he didn't have a way to communicate with the outside world? It seemed so wrong.

I turned my head and looked at a spot on the floor. "I guess I never thought about it that way."

He was up and hobbling toward me in an instant. "Hey, no! Stop that."

But everything became clear to me in that moment. Charlie needed the outside world. I didn't. I tossed my head, my hair flipping back. When he got to me, he reached to embrace me, I drew away.

"What are you doing, Matt?" He held his arms out. "Come here."

Oh, I wanted to. The few times he'd encircled me in his arms it actually seemed like they held the world at bay. They silenced the voices in my head, the fear that had always accompanied my incessant thinking.

"I need to go finish my canning," I replied softly, taking a few steps toward the kitchen.

"No! Come back!" he snarled, then lurched toward me, grunting in pain as he put weight on his leg. He went down, grabbing my shirt as he did. He dragged us both to the floor, him crying out as his leg twisted, and me in a state of panic because I'd caused him to be hurt.

I tried to scramble back, but he held tight. The thought of him in pain countermanded my fear of being held and unable to move. "Charlie!" I cried out.

"Okay, that hurt," he groaned, letting go of me and lying back on the floor.

"What the hell did you do that for?" I shouted. "You could have been hurt."

He chuckled and wrapped an arm over his ribs. "Oh, believe me, I was."

I got up on my knees and crawled over to him. "Let me see," I insisted as I tugged at his shirt. The skin over his ribs had turned a bright red, and I could see what looked to be a slight swelling. "I'm going to get some ice. Just stay here."

As I got up, he called my name. I stopped and stared at him.

"I'm sorry," he said softly.

"What for?" I asked as I opened the freezer and pulled out some frozen vegetables. I hurried back to him, knelt by his side, and placed the bag against his skin. He hissed, and I withdrew my hand.

"Cold!" he whimpered.

"Still a baby," I replied. "Hold this here."

He turned a pleading gaze toward me. "Can you stay here and hold it?"

"Yeah, for a bit. Then I'll get you a pain pill and put you to bed for a while."

He muttered something I didn't hear.

"What did you say?"

"Nothing important," he assured me.

My knees started to ache, so I sat beside him, rubbing the bag slowly over his skin. After a few minutes, I pulled the bag away, got up, and put it back in the freezer. I returned to where he still lay, held out my hand, and helped him up. He wrapped an arm around my shoulder, and together we moved toward the bedroom. After I got him comfortable on the bed, I got a glass of water and two of his pills, and took them back to him.

"I don't like these," he said petulantly.

"It'll help."

He sighed and grabbed the pills, popped them in his mouth, then washed them down with half the glass of water.

"Get some rest. I'll come check on you in a while." I went to the door and turned off the light.

"Matt?"

"Hmm?"

"Could you...?"

"What do you need?"

His voice was so soft, I had to strain to hear him. "Could you maybe stay a bit and read to me?"

There was no way a grown man had just asked me to read to him. I knew I must have misheard.

"Do you mind? Just for a little while. I… I don't really want to be alone."

Flicking the switch again, I turned the light back on. I smiled at him but noticed how pale he'd gotten. That fall must have taken a lot more out of him than he let on. "Sure. What do you want me to read?"

"*Death Comes to Allerton?*"

The innocent expression didn't fool me for a minute. "You just want to hear your own book."

"No, that's not it. I like the sound of your voice. I don't care what you read. I just want to hear you read it to me."

He gave me a small smile, and my heart pumped harder. I went to the other room and picked up the copy of the book he'd given me. When I got back to the bedroom, I pulled over a chair and sat next to him. He giggled like a little kid and scrunched down under the covers.

"My name is Donald Tremaine. Former soldier. Former cop. Currently a private detective, investigating the brutal death of Scott Tyler, a twenty-one-year-old man whose body was found cut up and placed into small bags, then dumped on the side of the highway…."

Before I got to the end of the first chapter, Charlie was asleep. I closed the book and returned it to its place on the bookshelf. I went back into the bedroom to ensure he was covered. I stood there for a moment, gazing at him. The warmth that flooded through me had me smiling. This had been the right decision, I was certain. I turned and put my hand up to switch the light off.

"Where are you going?" a sleepy voice asked.

"I'll be out there if you need me."

He crooked a finger. "I need you to come back here. Please?"

Thinking he might be in pain, I went to the bed and squatted down. "What's up?"

"Can you lie down with me? Just until I fall asleep?"

The hesitancy in his voice was so out of character for him, and it left me confused. "Charlie, is something wrong?"

He nodded as his eyes closed. "I don't like being alone in the bed. I want you to sleep with me. When you're not where I can see you, I miss you so much, it hurts."

I jumped up and stepped away from the bed. So many thoughts whirled around that I couldn't sort them out. I retreated to the living room and touched everything I owned, needing to find balance in my mind, but all I could hear were Charlie's words. I pulled out my phone and dialed Clay.

"Was starting to think since your new friend was staying there, you'd forgotten about me."

"I—He...." I swallowed hard.

"Charlie? What did he do?" Even though he was younger than me, Clay sounded very much like an angry big brother now.

"He wanted me to get in bed with him."

"He what!" Clay got so loud I had to pull the phone away from my ear for a moment.

"No, not like that," I hastened to explain. "He said... shit. This is coming out all wrong."

"It better be. Now explain to me, using small words, what the hell you're talking about."

So I did. Clay was quiet as I went through what happened.

"Matt," he growled. "You do *not* sleep with that man. I can't believe... you know what? I'm going to come pick him up. His sister is still at his place, so she can either take care of him or he can go back to New York."

I stared at my phone for a moment. I couldn't imagine why Clay was so angry. "What? No. He's not going anywhere. I want him to stay here. He didn't upset me. I just got nervous."

"Not the point. I'm leaving the office now. I'll be there shortly."

I sucked in a deep breath. "No."

"Excuse me?"

I could tell his temper was on the rise, but so was mine.

"I said no. I'm not a child. I invited him here, so he's staying. If—and let me stress *if*—I decide that I want to pursue a relationship

91

with him, that's my decision, not yours. I appreciate you trying to help, but you need to back off."

He sputtered, said a few curse words, and then hung up. I took several deep, satisfying breaths before I slipped my phone back into my pants. It felt good to finally stand up for myself, even if only for a few minutes. I waited to see if Clay would call back, and when he didn't, I went into the kitchen to put some things together in the Crock-Pot for tomorrow's lunch and dinner, then stepped outside. The air had turned bitter. I looked at the old thermometer that hung on the side of the greenhouse and shivered when I saw it showed three degrees, far below our average of forty. I was starting to get a bad feeling about this.

…WITH OVERNIGHT temperatures falling to minus eight and dropping throughout the week! We've got a snowstorm forming in Canada that might bring us an early Thanksgiving gift that we doubt anyone wants: Up to sixteen inches of snow, with another front that has the potential to drop even more a few days after. Get those long johns out, because you're gonna need them.

I switched the radio off, having learned everything I needed to know. The first powerful front of winter was bearing down on us weeks earlier than normal. I peeked into the bedroom. Charlie was still out, which was good. I had to make a decision. If the area was going to be buried by snow, then it might be best for Charlie to go back to town so he had access to the hospital, just in case something went wrong.

I fumbled with my phone when I took it out of my pocket. How much did it suck that I'd just told my brother off, and now I needed his help? I scrolled until his name came up and was ready to push the button when Charlie's voice came from the bedroom.

"Matt? Where are you?"

I put the phone down on the table and hurried to see what Charlie needed.

"Oh, I thought you might have gone out."

I tried really hard not to look at him like he was talking crazy. "Where would I go?"

"I don't know. Fishing?"

My chin dropped to my chest. Yeah, I wasn't thinking straight. Again. I should get dressed and go see about adding more provisions to the freezer.

"Hey, come here," he said, patting the edge of the bed.

I sat gingerly, ready to bolt if the need arose. He reached out and took my hand, wrapping his fingers in mine.

"How are you feeling?"

"To be honest, a little rough." He scratched his cheek and yawned. "Those pills really do a number on me."

I rubbed a thumb over the back of his hand, which seemed to calm both of us. "And your ribs?"

"As long as you don't make me laugh, I think I'll live."

"Well, then, it's a good thing I'm not funny."

He chuckled, then winced. "Yeah, you can be. Dry humor, but still makes me laugh." He smiled and I turned my head away. "Okay, what's wrong?"

"What do you mean?"

He cocked his head. "Really? You think after a few weeks of living here, I don't know your tells by now? You won't look me in the eye, so there's something bothering you. You're rubbing the back of my hand, so you're nervous and the contact soothes you. So make it better for both of us and tell me what's going on."

I made a sound in the back of my throat that was suspiciously like a whine. "I think you might need to go back to town."

He tried to sit up and pain flashed across his face. "Fuck!"

"Stop that. Just stay where you are."

He glared at me. "So you're telling me you want to get rid of me, and I'm supposed to just accept it? I thought things were going well." He sighed, seeming so sad. "I'll go if you want me to, but can you at least tell me why?"

"We've got a storm coming. Looks like it's going to be a bad one," I explained.

"Okay, still not seeing what that has to do with anything."

93

"You fell this morning and got hurt. If something were to happen while you were here, we couldn't get you to the hospital. And you've got your appointment in a few weeks to get checked out."

He hummed. "Okay, I'm missing something here." He struggled to adjust himself on the bed. "I did something stupid and paid the price. There's a storm coming, which I assume is a snowstorm, and you think I'm better off in town. Does that about cover it?"

When he said it like that, it did sound somewhat ridiculous. I tried to stand, but he tightened his grip on my hand.

"Oh no. I can't chase after you, so you need to stay where you're at."

I stared at our joined hands. Charlie was so unlike other people. They scared me. He… made me feel safe.

I needed to make him understand the situation. "I live miles from town. I don't have a vehicle. Then there's the fact that this is a pretty treacherous road—as you're no doubt aware—and we've got snow coming. If the weather service is right, a lot of snow. What do you think is going to happen?"

Charlie gave a light shrug of one shoulder. "The town will plow. What's the big deal?"

"On the ninth of January, we got nine inches of snow."

"Right. It was sloppy, wet, and heavy. I helped to shovel out some of the neighbors."

A quick sigh. Eventually he'd understand where I was going with this. "The weather didn't get much above freezing. That snow didn't melt from the roads around here until mid-February."

His eyes flashed, and I knew he'd finally figured it out.

"You're saying they won't plow up here."

"Exactly. I'm one person, living alone. My road doesn't see much traffic, so they're not important. The town won't do anything out here. Every winter up here, I settle in, because I won't be going anywhere."

Charlie frowned as if he were deep in thought about what I'd just said. Then he looked up at me and smiled. "I still don't see the problem here. If I'm going to be stuck somewhere, I'd rather it be with someone I like. Besides, it sounds romantic, don't you think?"

I just gawped.

94

CHAPTER ELEVEN

"THIS ISN'T a joke," I finally snapped. "We've had storms where I couldn't get out of the house for a week because the snow had piled high against the door. The only thing that works in my favor is that I've planned for it. I don't schedule chores outside during the winter, because there is no way I can know if they'll get done. So when things get crappy outside, I'm inside, warm and content with my books. I take a lot of naps. I cook, clean, and pick through the seeds I harvested in the fall for planting in spring."

Charlie lay there and looked at me for several moments. "Oh, you're done? Sorry. I was waiting for the downside to this."

I couldn't understand this man at all. He infuriated me, and for some reason, I didn't mind it. Heaven help me, I *liked* it. For the first time in my life, I felt… well, seminormal… ish. Yes, Charlie did things that irritated me, but so had my mom and brother, and I still lived with them for two years after the incident. But Charlie was… I didn't know how to explain it. He was so very different. He never got angry at me. With me, perhaps, but there was a difference. He didn't lash out or scream at me. He talked to me in measured tones. I knew it was to keep me from freaking out, and I appreciated that.

Having him in the house had opened my eyes. I'd thought after I left home, I could never be with anyone again. But having Charlie here made me appreciate what having him nearby meant. He'd offer to help with my projects. More often than not, I said no, but I found myself saying yes to some small things. I loved watching him try to shuck seeds with his hand in a splint. He made an absolute mess, but I laughed instead of freaking out. I—no, best not to go there. This was only to help him out, and it wouldn't—couldn't—ever be anything more.

"You're thinking too much," he said as he tugged me closer. "Lie down, Matt. I promise I won't do anything. I just want you to be by me."

He let go of my hand, and I stood. I looked into his eyes and saw nothing but warmth. I stepped around to the other side of the bed and lay atop the comforter. He reached for my hand again, clasping it in his.

"I wasn't kidding, you know. I don't like it when I can't see you or hear you. I don't understand how you do it. To me, the house is too lonely without your presence in it. In town, I didn't mind being alone. Here? I need you, Matt. You make this place more than a house—you make it a home."

He squeezed my fingers gently. As much as I wanted to, I couldn't help but turn my head toward him. His smile called to me, made me want things I couldn't explain. His lips were a soft pink, and I found myself moving closer to him. My hand was on his chest, my face moving closer. He put his fingers in my hair and held me against him.

"Listen."

"To what?"

"Close your eyes and listen."

I did as he asked. I closed my eyes and let the familiar sounds of my home and land surround me. I could hear the winds picking up, the sounds of the birds huddled in the trees as they waited for the weather to clear so they could gobble the seeds I'd left them, the sleet pelting against the windows. I started to move, but he kept a hand lightly stroking my hair.

"I don't know what you want me to hear."

"Then you aren't listening close enough. Try again, okay?"

With a heavy sigh at this wasted time, I did as he asked.

"You're making this a project when it doesn't need to be, Matt. Just let go and trust yourself and me."

For several minutes I still heard nothing. Frustration welled up inside of me, and I was about to tell him the whole thing was an exercise in futility when I heard it. A steady rhythm thudded gently in my ear, strong, dependable. I gasped.

"You hear it?"

Unable to speak, I nodded. I'd never heard another person's heart beating. I had no idea why this had such an impact on me, but it did. Charlie's clean scent, the feeling of the shirt fabric brushing against my face, the sound of his heartbeat, and the comfort I felt from all of them. It was too much. I sat up and stared at him.

"You look surprised."

"Why did you ask me to do that?"

"Because I wanted you to hear the sound of my heart. You're a person who appreciates consistency, and that's probably the one organ in the body that always keeps going. Well, in theory, anyway. But my reasons for asking you to listen were selfish. I want you to know that you can depend on me too. Just like my heart, I'm going to keep going on and on."

He reached out and put a hand on my cheek. He guided me toward him, and for a split second, I wanted to pull away. I didn't, though. I let him guide me to where he wanted me. We were face-to-face, millimeters apart, and then it happened. Our lips touched ever so gently. He didn't force it or try to take it deeper. He simply lay there with his lips pressed to mine. I reached a hand up and touched his face. He hadn't shaved today, and his skin felt rough, prickly. But I liked it. I pushed in a little more, and he moaned. His mouth opened slightly, and I felt his tongue touch the crease of my lips. My mind struggled to catch up from the overwhelming sensations. I let his tongue slide in and touch mine. He tasted sweet, like sugar candy. Lightning striking me couldn't have shocked me more. My cock surged to life, pressing against my pants. I wanted—no, I *needed*—him to touch me, to show me what I'd missed out on all these years.

"Charlie," I gasped.

He pulled back slightly and looked me in the eyes. "Did you like that?"

I nodded mutely.

"I did too. You're quite the kisser, you know."

My face heated, and he chuckled.

"Can we do that again?" I asked, trying to maintain my poise so I didn't start begging him for more kisses.

"As often as you like," he promised, sliding his fingers along the back of my neck.

"And more?"

He scrunched his face up. "I'm not sure if you're ready for more, and to be honest, I don't know that I am either. You're not someone who you meet and take back to your room for a quickie. You deserve better. And I want to give that to you. I want to give you my heart, Matt, because, of everyone I know in the world, I think it's safest with you."

What I did next, I never expected of myself. I lay beside him, with my head on his chest and my arm wrapped around his waist. It was the most intimate thing I'd ever done, and instead of freaking about it, I sank into the feelings.

Charlie kissed my hair, then whispered to me, "I'd really like it if you could try to sleep in the bed with me. I like having you here, where I can keep an eye on you."

I jerked up, sputtering indignantly. "I'll have you know, I don't need anyone to watch me. I've been perfectly fine for more than a decade."

He smiled at me. "You're a little spitfire, aren't you, Matt? Wanna know what I like best about you? After everything that's happened to you, you're still so strong. But have you considered I'm not doing this for you, and maybe it's for me? Maybe having you near me settles something within *me*. We all have things we hold on to, stuff we need to settle the terror within us. Mine happens to be being here, with you. It gives me peace of mind. It makes me whole again."

There was nothing I could say to that. It was the same for me. Having Charlie here meant everything, and I didn't want him to leave. I'd never thought that I could live with someone, but now I was finding out that I was more afraid of living without someone.

"So don't make me go. Please? Whatever happens, we'll deal with it, I promise."

I glanced up and saw him looking down at me. His expression made my chest tighten.

"Hey."

"Hi."

It pretty much sucked as witty repartee, but it wasn't the words as much as the emotions behind them. I was scooting closer, intent on kissing him again, when I heard a car outside the house. I sat up and peered out the window. "Fuck. It's my brother," I muttered.

Charlie tensed, which seemed unusual.

"Listen, Matt, there's something I should tell you—"

98

"In a minute. I have to go see what he wants."

I pushed off the bed and walked out of the bedroom, closing the door behind me. I opened the front door, wanting to see why the hell Clay was here. Charlie kept trying to call me back, but I already saw Clay stomping toward me.

He pushed his way into the house, which set off my anxiety. "Where the hell is he?" he demanded.

"He's in bed. He fell and hurt himself."

Clay snorted. "I'm gonna do more than hurt him."

He stormed toward the bedroom, brushing me aside when I tried to block him. Charlie was up, wobbling on his feet when Clay entered the bedroom. The expression on Clay's face terrified me. I'd never seen him filled with so much rage before.

"What the fuck do you think you're doing?"

Charlie held up a hand. "Clay, think about what you're going to say before you open your mouth."

"Oh, I know damn well what I'm going to say. You stay the hell away from Matt."

"Excuse me? I think it's my choice—" I tried to interject, but Clay turned his anger toward me, and I withered.

"I want you out of his house," he growled at Charlie. "Now."

"No," Charlie replied, his tone showing a stubborn streak to match Clay's.

Clay stalked toward Charlie and jabbed a finger into his chest, almost knocking him down. "You were supposed to get him out of here and back to town. Not play house with him! How can he ever get better if you're feeding into his fantasies?"

Charlie's gaze flicked to me, and in that moment, everything became clear as crystal. This had all been a setup. Charlie wasn't here because he wanted me; he'd come because Clay had…. Goddammit. They'd played me for a fool.

"You set this up," I said quietly. "Both of you. Now I get it. This was all bullshit."

Charlie shook his head harshly. "No, Matt, I—"

I didn't want to listen to any more lies now that I knew why he'd been so nice to me, why he'd worked so hard to get me to trust him. Fuck, I'd been so stupid. "Get out. Both of you."

Charlie took a few tentative steps toward me, but I kept out of his reach. "Matt, let me explain—"

"You know what's funny?" I said, tears staining my cheeks. "I thought maybe, for the first time in my life, I'd finally found something real. Something I could build on. Who knew that it was all a lie? Well, obviously you and my brother."

The two men now glared at each other, Clay puffing like an angry bull.

"I want you both to leave now," I said, as calmly as I could. "I don't want to see either of you again."

"Matt, no—" Charlie said, looking absolutely stricken.

"Get the fuck out of my house!" I shrieked, glaring at Charlie. "Get out. Take your shit with you and just go."

Clay folded his arms across his chest, a smug expression on his face.

I turned and simply stared at him. "I hope you're happy, Clay. You've destroyed everything I thought I could have. Now? Thanks to you, there's nothing left. Congratulations, you've ruined my life."

His smile faded. He turned toward me and tried to speak. "What? No, that's not—"

"Please leave," I said wearily. "Just go."

Both of them spoke at once, trying to get me to hear them out. I was tired of listening to other people. It only led to heartache.

"I'm going down to the pond," I said. Despite the crappy conditions outside, it was better than being here with them. "I expect you both to be gone before I get back."

Clay grabbed my arm. "Matt, you have to listen—"

"To what?" I shouted, jerking away. "More lies? I can't believe you set this whole thing up. I thought you loved me."

"I do!" he protested. "I wanted—"

"What you wanted doesn't matter. Go back to town where you belong. Don't bother trying to talk to Judge Hamlin, because I'll

100

tell him what you've done. I'm pretty sure he'd sign a permanent restraining order for me. Just leave me alone. I don't want either of you to contact me again." And with that, I grabbed my heavy coat, hat, and scarf and went to the door. "Goodbye, Charlie," I whispered as I stepped out into the wet, snowy weather.

THE WINDS howled down by my pond, sloshing water over the shore. The sleet lashed at my face and eyes, even through my scarf. It was nearly impossible to see, and there was no way I could fish in this weather. But I didn't want to return to the scene of my humiliation. I sat on a rock and stared into the water, wondering how I could have been so foolish. I'd actually been ready to tell Charlie I loved him, to let him into my life fully. Yeah, that was stupid on my part. Apparently the only way someone would want to be with me was when they were trying to get me out of my home.

According to my watch, an hour had passed since I left Charlie and Clay. Should have been plenty of time for them to have gotten the hell out. I drew my jacket tighter and headed through the woods toward home. The sun was just dipping below the horizon, which made the walk extra shitty. I slid more than once, nearly took a tumble that would have sent me back down the hill I'd just climbed, and found it really hard to care. I wasn't self-destructive, but then again, I didn't need to be. I had enough people in my life who were willing to hurt me, so I pushed on.

The house was dark as I approached. Clay's truck was gone, and I breathed a sigh of relief. I really didn't feel like getting into it with him again. I couldn't believe he could do something like this. All his words about loving me, helping me. All lies. And Charlie was worse. He'd made me trust him, believe in him. Hell, he'd made me believe in myself. I'd actually thought that I might be worth loving and that what Mr. Jackson had done to me didn't make me tainted.

The sleet and rain began to change to snow. Big, sloppy, wet flakes hit the ground and joined others of their kind. The white blanket that came every year had once again started to cover my home. I pushed the door open and stepped inside. It was almost as cold and dark as outside, with all the warmth I'd associated with the place having been sucked out. Yet, there was still that sense of urgency that Charlie wasn't here that left me off-kilter. He'd become so engrained in the place, I couldn't accept the fact that he wasn't there.

I went around the room, touching all my items. When I got to the shelf with Charlie's books, my hand trembled. I couldn't be sure I'd come back from this betrayal, but at the same time, I hurt that he was gone. Even more than what he'd done to me, his loss had left me bereft.

I made several passes through the house, handling everything, trying to ground myself again. I no longer had a center, and felt as though I was falling. If this was what love meant, I was glad I'd never said the words. But Charlie was still in my mind and my heart. Everything in me ached.

The fire I'd started earlier had long burned down and now was nothing more than cold gray ash. I added new kindling and a few logs, then ignited it. It wasn't as strong as the earlier fire, but it didn't matter. Charlie needed the heat. I didn't. Me? I was tired and needed sleep. I looked toward the bedroom, but I couldn't be in there tonight. Maybe never again. I curled up on the couch, the firelight casting shadows around the room. It was almost nine, and if I could, I think I would have just slept forever. But by ten I still hadn't fallen asleep. I got up, made some decaf, and sat staring into the fire.

The sound of an approaching vehicle had me out of my seat and rushing for the window. It could only be Clay, and I didn't want to see him. Imagine my surprise when a truck I'd never seen before came to a jerky stop and the door swung open. I couldn't call Clay and wasn't sure what to do. Then I breathed a sigh of relief as Charlie slid from the cab, barely able to catch himself on the seat before he fell to the ground.

I rushed outside and found him struggling to keep his footing. "What the hell's wrong with you?" I shouted over the wind that whipped through the area.

He looked up at me with sad eyes, but he grinned. "Aren't you going to invite me in?"

"Hell no. I told you I didn't want to see you anymore."

He gestured toward himself. "And yet, here I am. I drove all this way to talk to you, so the least you can do is let me sit down."

I put my hands on my hips. "No. Go away."

Charlie shrugged. "Okay, if you really want me driving back down that ice- and snow-covered road, then I guess I'll go."

Memories of the last time flooded my mind. I'd said goodbye, and he'd had an accident. The thought that I would never see him again had me running for the house. I needed something to tether me, because right now I was falling apart. I didn't know how much time passed, but I heard the door close and Charlie hobbling up behind me.

His arms, so strong, wrapped around my waist. I couldn't help myself. I turned and clung to him, because right now, he was the only thing that was real. The only thing I could hold on to. Even though I hated how weak I was, I needed Charlie to give me strength, to help return my life.

"Don't leave me," I whispered as I buried my face into his chest.

"I won't," he promised as he encircled me in his arms.

CHAPTER TWELVE

THE WINDS were the first thing I noticed as I came awake. The second was being in bed, with the comforter around me and a weight across my chest. I turned my head to the side and my stomach clenched when I realized I was in bed with Charlie. I pushed his arm off me and bolted from the bed.

He blinked open his eyes and smiled at me. "Good morning. Coffee ready?"

"Get out," I snarled.

The memories came back slowly. Last night I'd needed him so much. When he led me to the bedroom, I thought it was a dream. He laid me down and covered me, then crawled in beside me. He spooned me, and his warmth allowed me to sleep. But today the anger surged back.

"Have you looked outside?" he asked. "I did about two hours ago when I got up to use the bathroom. The snowdrifts almost cover the truck. So I'm kind of stuck here. I mean, unless you want me to hobble back down to town. Which should only take until I freeze to death."

He was trying to play on my sympathies, and the bastard knew I wouldn't send him out.

"Why are you here? No, wait. How did you even get here?"

He shrugged one shoulder. "Your brother drove me back to town. Suffice it to say he wasn't happy about the situation. He didn't say a word to me until he got to my place. That's when he let me have it. He told me I'd turned you against him, how I'd messed you up even more, and that I should, quote, 'get the fuck out of Fall Harbor.' Then he pretty much kicked me and my stuff to the curb. When I got to the door, Teresa was *pissed off*. She yelled at me and called me quite a few colorful names, but I think a lot of that had to do with the weather. She always gets cranky when it snows." He rolled over on his side and leveled his gaze at me. "As soon as I got into the house, I grabbed her keys and told her I was coming back here. She took them from me and refused to let me leave the house. So I waited until she fell asleep, took them from her purse, and here I am. Driving was a pain. You never notice how much you depend on your right foot until you can't use it. But I was determined to get back here, because I couldn't let things end. Not like that."

"Why did you come back? You should have just stayed in town. It would have been better for both of us."

He pushed himself up until he was leaning against the headboard. "For you, maybe. It wouldn't have been better for me. You might want to sit down for this, because it's going to be a long story. Actually, we might want to eat first, because I'm famished."

I narrowed my gaze at him. "Get on with it."

A much put-upon sigh was my reply. The bastard was milking this.

"At least come back to bed. It's cold, and you generate a lot of body heat."

My stomach roiled at his statement. He wasn't wrong. My teeth were already chattering. I opened the closet and pulled out another comforter, which I wrapped around myself. The heavy down immediately began to warm me. I sat on the chair from the desk and stared at him.

"You may not believe me, but I did try to tell you before Clay showed up. I don't want to lie to you about anything."

"No, the two of you would rather just plot behind my back," I snapped.

"It's not like that," Charlie assured me. "Maybe after I explain, you'll understand." He took a deep breath and closed his eyes briefly. When he opened them again, he leveled his gaze at me, holding my complete attention. "About a year and a half ago, not long after I arrived, Clay came into the library. Like I said. I was pretty new here, and I was looking up town facts—weather, precipitation, and things like that. Clay struck up a conversation, and I found him to be funny and friendly. We started meeting for coffee at the Clover a couple times a week. Anyway, after about a month or so, he mentioned he's got a brother who lives far out of town. When I asked him why, he said you had your reasons and they weren't for him to tell me."

I leaned forward because I wanted to hear more. Yesterday I was angry at Clay, but it had simmered into a deep hurt. I knew Clay loved me, and sometimes he did stupid things, but he was my brother. Charlie was another matter entirely. How well did I really know him? Months of jogging by my house, and a few times with a bit of conversation? Did that really let me understand him at all?

"Every time we talked, he would mention you. How proud he was that you'd made a life for yourself, how incredible you were, and so forth. I admit, I was intrigued. The more we met, the more I learned. The more I found out, the more I wanted to know. Finally Clay tells me where you live, but he also mentions you're shy around people you don't know, and that if I wanted to meet you, I had to let you come to me."

The bastard made me sound like a wounded animal? Yet it worked, didn't it? He got me to talk to Charlie, and he got my guard down.

"So I asked him how he thought I should go about it. He knew I liked to run. I would do it every day in town, and more than once, he saw me as he was driving by. So he suggested I start running down this road. He said your nature would win out eventually. So I figured, why not? He was very specific that if I was going to do it, it would need to be at the same time every day, and that if I deviated from my schedule, you would panic."

Okay, how had I not known that Clay knew me so well? A chill went through me. I wrapped myself tighter in the comforter, but that only dulled it.

Charlie reached out a hand, and I took it. "Come back to bed, Matt."

My mind fuzzed out. I got up, threw the comforter on the bed, and then crawled in beside Charlie. Though I worried he would try to kiss me again, he merely reached down and laced his fingers with mine.

"I started coming up here, mostly out of curiosity. But then I noticed you watching me from your window, and I... I don't know. I was drawn to the shy man who needed to be the one to approach me. One day, I figured I'd let you know I wasn't here to hurt you, so I waved. Your eyes went wide and you ducked down. You were so freaking adorable. I had a smile on my face the rest of my run."

Adorable? I squeezed his hand hard, so he could see how *adorable* I was. The smug bastard smiled and squeezed back, though not hard enough to hurt.

"When I talked to Clay that afternoon, I told him what had happened. Now this is where the story might get uncomfortable for you, but please, try to keep in mind that Clay and your mom love you very, very much."

My mom? Shit. What did she have to do with this?

"I got invited to dinner that night. When I met your mom, she hugged me and welcomed me into her home. When Clay explained to her who I was, she flashed me a smile and told me she'd read one of my books. That made me feel ten feet tall. As she was putting the food together, Clay told me the reason why he wanted me to get you out. He said he worried about you, out here alone. He said he hoped that if you got comfortable with me, you'd come back to town. I was angry because I felt like he was using me, and I told him so. But then your mom came back into the room, and she said she hasn't spoken to you for years. I didn't understand that, but when Clay tried to explain, I told him I didn't want to hear it from him. I only wanted to hear your story from you. And to do that, I needed to keep coming back."

I cleared my throat and looked away from him. If I expected to get to know Charlie, then I had to let him know the real me, warts and all.

"I love my mom," I started. "After the incident, she got overbearing. She insisted I go to see a doctor, and when that didn't work, she tried to make me go into a hospital. I tried to tell her there was nothing wrong with me, but she wouldn't listen. One day we got into an argument about it. She said I could get help, that I could be *normal* again. When she realized what she'd said, she tried to apologize, but…. The damage was done. I knew then she didn't see me as Matt anymore, but as someone broken. I started to notice things. Clay looked at me with pity in his eyes. He stopped bringing people over, which was good for me, but I felt like he was resentful toward me. As soon as I hit eighteen and the settlement came through, I contacted my lawyer and authorized him to make the purchase for this land."

I turned to Charlie, desperate for someone to *finally* understand.

107

"I know she loves me, and I love her, but it was like… I don't know, we were all trapped in these roles, and there wasn't a way to get out of them. It got to the point where every time I looked at them, I could see pity in both their eyes, and I couldn't take it anymore. Clay gets mad because I don't call, but every time I do, the conversation goes the same: 'When are you going back to the doctor?' or 'I don't understand why you can't live in town.'"

"They worry, Matt. They care about you, and they want you back in their lives."

I opened my mouth to protest, because he didn't get it, and he held a hand up.

"But I understand why you moved out here. It's beautiful. Peaceful. Even in a small town, there's going to be a lot of hustle and bustle. Out here? You can be alone with your thoughts."

Yes! That was exactly how I felt. The solitude was calming to me. But more than once, I'd found myself wondering what it would be like if I lived closer to town. I'd actually had a dream where Charlie came over and picked me up to take me to a nearby town with a movie theater. We'd sit and watch something inane, each have a soda and popcorn, and he'd hold my hand. No one would give us a second look, and when we walked out of the theater, he'd put his arm around me and hold me close.

"I'm going to tell you something, and I want you to know that this is the God's honest truth. Yes, Clay and your mother were hoping that I would be able to talk you into coming back to town. I didn't know about the therapy until you told me. But here's the thing. Once I got out here, ran the roads, met you, and saw what you've accomplished here? I don't want you to come back to town."

I gasped and tried to draw away, but Charlie held me tight.

"Listen to me. I don't want you to do anything that makes you uncomfortable. If this is where you're happiest, then you need to be here, but—and Matt, this is important—if you'll have me, I want to be here with you. I love it out here. The times I ran, I felt freer than I ever had. It's why, when I met you, I was hoping you'd see me. And so you know, it's not just the land that makes me feel free."

He leaned closer and kissed my forehead.

108

"I love you, Matt."

My chest constricted and I could scarcely breathe. What would I do if I woke up and realized it was a dream? I'd known how I felt about Charlie since he was in the hospital. It was what got my ass out of the house and into town to see him. The thought caused my stomach to flutter. Charlie had been all over the United States doing book tours. He had wanted his ex to go with him, but his ex wouldn't. That had caused problems in their relationship. And while I would never cheat on Charlie, would he be disappointed that I couldn't go?

I looked up into his eyes, and they twinkled in the light.

"What are you thinking?"

"Would you ask me to go with you on book tours?"

He smiled. "Sweetheart, anywhere I go, you would be welcome at my side. Don't think that means you have to. I'm serious. If you're comfortable here, if you feel safe, then you should be here. I will always come home to you. And, if you think that my being away would be problematic, then I simply won't go. Tours are only to promote the books, and if I'm honest, I don't really care much for the travel that comes with them. If I'm going to go somewhere, I want it to be a place I'd like to visit with someone special."

I scanned his face, trying to see if he was being completely honest. I couldn't see anything that told me he wasn't.

"I want to go with you," I whispered. "I love it here, but...." How could I tell him what was in my heart? He was the writer. I didn't have the words for it. "I realized that it's just a place to be. It wasn't a home until you came along. You gave it warmth—no, you gave *me* warmth. For the first time in my life, I wasn't afraid. And having you here? I realized that my collection wasn't the only thing that gave me inner peace. You did that too."

His chest puffed up a little. "What are you saying?"

I bit my lip. God, I wished I was better at talking. "I love you. I want to be with you, but I can't ask you to give up your life like that."

"Hey, it would be my—"

"No," I said flatly, dipping my chin. "You might think that it sounds good now, but trust me, I've been here more than a decade. It's beautiful, but I never realized it was lonely too. I'm tired of being alone. Of being afraid." I snuggled in closer to him, loving the warmth from his body. "Where is the most exciting place you've ever been?"

"Right here, right now" came the husky answer. "That's what you don't get. There is nowhere in the world I've been that is better than where we are right now. I could live here with you happily for the rest of my life. We don't need to change a thing. Well, maybe the sheets once in a while."

I knew he was trying to defuse the situation with humor, but I didn't need that anymore. What I wanted was Charlie. Always Charlie. But was I trading one problem for another? What if he left me? Would I be able to survive it?

"Matt?"

"Yes?" I met his gaze, and he kissed me until I grew light-headed. When he pulled back, I glared at him. "Why did you do that?"

"Because you wanted me to. You're imagining all the worst-case scenarios. Thinking about every conceivable problem. Am I saying it's going to be easy? No. I know better. But do I think it will be worth it to try? Absolutely. See, your brother may have nudged me in your direction, but you kept me here. Your smile, your charm, your wit. Everything about you calls to me."

"Are you sure you're not just in love with being in love again?"

Charlie chuckled. "When I was with Mitch, I wanted it all—the travel, the semifame that came with being an author, the pretty decent paycheck, and the boy toy at my side. But with you? I want exactly that. You. If I never wrote another book again, I'd have something in my life that made me feel settled and at peace. Let me put it to you this way: the thought of laying outside with you, watching the galaxy stretched before me, and then having a swarm of insects come out and wiggle their butts? I want that. More than I think I've ever wanted anything.

"I know I'm not exactly who you thought I was, and I get that you're angry with me and your brother. Keep in mind, though, without him, I never would have found you. After we left yesterday, he yelled at me a lot, until I told him I was in love with you. That shut him up. At least for a minute. But Clay was angry because he cares. When he found out my true feelings, he stopped and listened. I explained to him what you meant to me. What being here with you did for me. And I told him there is nothing wrong with you. If you're happy, how can it be wrong? I said maybe it wasn't you who needed to change, but him and your mother. *Then* he kicked me to the curb."

I shook my head. "No. It's not just them. I need to meet them halfway. I think I've always known it, but I was afraid. Being with you, I'm not so scared anymore. That doesn't mean I'm ever going to be normal—"

"Stop that," Charlie snapped, flicking a finger against my forehead. "What is normal? Who decides?"

"I miss my mom."

His grip around me tightened. "She misses you too. Maybe you just need to show her that you're okay. I think that's what she worries most about."

I took a deep, shuddering breath. Every insecurity I had, Charlie had seen. And he still wanted me. If he could do this for me, what could I do for him?

"I want to go back to therapy," I said, my voice surprisingly solid.

"Are you sure?"

I nodded, rubbing my chin over his chest. "I don't know what good it's going to do me, but I want to try. To see my mom again. My brother. To go places and do things with you? Yeah, I'm sure. And, if you still want to, I'd like to have you here with me. This could be your home too."

Charlie sighed. "I want to. More than you could ever know." He twirled a finger in my hair. "I told you, this place felt like coming home for me. I wasn't kidding. I've never in my life felt more comfortable anywhere. Never had it bother me that I left it. But yesterday, when you told me to go? I couldn't walk away. I had to come back, because I gave you my heart. You're the only one who was ever meant to have it."

Fuck. How could I say no to this soppy, romantic man? And why the hell would I ever think I wanted to?

CHAPTER THIRTEEN

THE STORM was every bit as bad as they'd said. We got almost two feet of snow that was blown into huge drifts. It was okay, though. The light powder gave me the perfect opportunity to introduce Charlie to one of my favorite things. I went outside, armed with the down comforters I had in storage. I placed them on the swing, then shoveled away what snow had accumulated on the porch to make room. Afterward, I went back in, took Charlie by the arm, led him out to the swing, sat down with him, and covered us up.

"Shit," he whispered, looking at the tens of thousands of refractions of sunlight sparkling off the fresh snow. "I'll admit, I'm not sure I've ever seen something so beautiful." He turned to me. "Well, except you."

I nudged him gently with my elbow. "Stop that."

"Never going to happen," he promised. "I'm going to make sure that every day of your life, you know exactly how important you are to me. I was stupid for not telling you about Clay, but to be honest, once I met you, it didn't really come into my head again. All that was there was you."

Little feathers tickled my stomach.

He waved a hand toward the horizon. "Your land is amazing. It's so much like you. There are things you can see with your eyes, but the important stuff isn't on the surface. You need to look deeper, see beneath it all. Dig up the things that lie hidden underneath."

"My mother always says, 'butter wouldn't melt in your mouth.' She must have been talking about you."

"Aw, that's sweet. I think." He cocked his head and narrowed his eyes. "Wait. Is that a compliment or an insult?"

I laughed, and it felt good. The tension that had bound my chest eased slightly.

"We're going to have to talk to your brother," Charlie said. "I don't want him coming out here again and upsetting you."

Resisting the urge to squint at him, I said, "Him? You both pissed me off. I can't believe he set this whole thing up."

Charlie gave a one-shoulder shrug. "He gave me a little push in this direction. Believe me, if you hadn't intrigued me so much, I wouldn't have kept coming back." He reached his hand out and cupped my cheek. "And you *so* very much intrigue me."

I found myself pressing into his touch. His hand warmed my cheek, even in the bitter cold. He rubbed my cheek for a bit, then leaned against the swing.

"Do you want to go back in?" I asked.

"Not unless you want to. I want to sit here and soak in the peace and tranquility. If someone had told me something like this would call to me, I'd have said they were crazy. But it does. I want to see the seasons as they change. To watch as the snow melts away and the blooms of spring burst up from the ground. I remember seeing your flowers when I would run by. Their gentle scent filled the air, and after a while, I noticed I went slower as I passed.

"After a few weeks, I desperately wanted to meet you. This tract of land showed that someone loved it, gave it form and beauty. When I saw you hiding in there, watching me, I felt some strange connection to you. I thought about coming to your door and knocking, but remembered that you had to come to me. And the day you did? After I got out of sight, I pumped my fist, I was so damn happy."

When I coughed and looked away, he tapped me on the leg.

"What are you thinking?"

No way did I want to do this. "I only came out to talk to you because Clay blackmailed me. He said if I didn't, he would see about getting me consigned to a hospital."

Instead of being angry, Charlie laughed. "I'm grateful for it, then. He knew you needed a push, and he did it in a way that still gave you the power."

"He pissed me off," I snapped.

"But it got you to talk to me. And believe me, it was worth it." He nestled closer and put his head on my shoulder.

I took in a deep breath and found myself at peace. "I love you."

113

He moved slightly and kissed my neck, which caused goose bumps to pebble on my skin. "Love you too," he murmured.

WE DID get a second weather wallop a few days later. Another storm from Canada pushed toward us, dropping six more inches of snow. The thing of it was, neither of us minded being in the house. Charlie sat at his computer, typing away, while I did my chores, and after I was done, I read another one of his books. Every so often, I would peer up and see him thoughtfully biting the end of the pen he'd use to jot down notes, his computer receiving his full concentration.

Or so I thought.

"You know, it's not fair," he said.

"What's that?"

"You're sitting there licking your lips while you look at me, and I can't take you to bed."

Take me to bed? My breath must have hitched, because Charlie gave me a soft smile.

"Sorry. I don't want to push it. But, so you know, I do dream about it. You under me, over me, in me. I want you in every way imaginable, Matt. But I'm patient, and when you're ready and comfortable, we'll take it slow."

In him? "You mean you want…?"

He gave me the sweetest smile as he shook his head. "Why does that surprise you so much? My ex swore he didn't bottom. Me? Love it. Also love topping. And siding. And sucking. Oh, and swallowing. I bet you taste delicious."

My head spun and my face burned. When I dreamed of it, I always thought that Charlie would be the one who was doing… that. I never expected he'd want me to. I swallowed hard. Fuck, now that I had the thought in my head, my cock leaped up with interest.

"What are you doing?" I asked, trying to change the subject.

"Smooth," Charlie teased. He turned back to his computer. "I'm working on book seven. It's going to be titled *Comes a Foul Wind*. It deals with Lucien finding a decayed corpse while he's out walking the

114

dogs. He goes to Donald, who rushes down to the lake, only to find no evidence there was ever a body there in the first place."

"Can I read it?" I practically begged, not giving a damn that I had no shame.

Charlie shook his head. "Sorry. It's in my contract that my publisher and editor have to see all copy first. If I show it to you, I'd be in trouble."

It made sense, and I sure didn't want him to risk his job for me. Even though I really wanted to read it, like, now.

"The good news? I'm almost done with it. It's taken me over a year, during which time my publisher has been hounding me for the book. I'm figuring another week and it'll be ready to go to them. Hopefully it'll be out by Christmas next year."

"But that's so far away," I complained. "Can you at least tell me what happens?"

He got up and hobbled over to where I sat, took a seat next to me, and leaned in close. His warm breath on my ear caused me to shudder. "Nope," he whispered.

I drew back, squinted at him, and barked out, "You're mean!"

He nodded enthusiastically. "Yeah, I know."

"Come on," I whined, reaching out to take his hand. "Just a hint."

If pressed, I would admit I had rarely ever been so excited before. Charlie built a world that I would love to live in—well, okay, maybe with a few less deaths—and knowing that I had him here, in my house, and teasing me? I wanted to scream. In a good way, of course. Plus, I'd made it through all six books and had started to read them over again.

"Let's just say that this book is going to come as a huge surprise to a lot of people."

"I hate you," I grumbled.

He leaned over and whispered in my ear, "That's okay. You'll get over it." Charlie laughed at me when he found me glaring. He put a hand on my cheek, stroking it slowly. "You're simply adorable, do you know that?"

That caused me to narrow my gaze. "Yes, because everyone wants to be adorable."

I tried to pull back, but Charlie put his hand on my chin. "Hey, there is nothing wrong with being adorable." He kissed my forehead— "Or sweet."—my nose—"Or beautiful."—my lips.

Damn. My cock rose to full erection once more. Charlie's scent, clean and masculine, wrapped around me. He leaned as close as he could and put his lips to my neck, and goose bumps rose on my arms.

"Tell me this is okay, Matt," he whispered. "I won't do anything if you say it's not."

My throat closed up. He wouldn't push me, had no desire to make me feel uncomfortable. What he'd said before was true. He wanted me to be happy.

"Yes," I murmured. "Please."

I could hear the smile in his voice when he said, "I like it when you say please. Take off your shirt for me."

I stood up and stripped off my flannel shirt, and Charlie's breathing grew husky.

"T-shirt too, please."

"But it's cold," I whined.

"T-shirt too, please," he repeated.

My skin pebbled after I stripped the shirt off. Charlie patted the couch, and I sat next to him. He trailed his hand slowly down my chest, circling my nipples, which were so hard they throbbed. Every nerve ending stood on end, in hopes that he'd somehow touch it next. He slid his fingertips over my stomach, which tensed slightly. He stopped immediately, not moving until I relaxed. Then he continued his exploration. When he brushed his hand against my groin, I moaned and reflexively thrust up to meet it.

"Has anyone ever touched you?" he asked, his voice full of determination.

"Me. Lots of times. Well, at least when I was a horny teenager."

"Oh, Matt," he purred. "There are so many things I want to explore with you. So many firsts I want to be a part of."

"Like what?" I groaned, needing to hear his voice.

"I want to suck you until you come in my mouth. I want you to take me to bed and fuck me slow, hard, deep, shallow—any way

116

you want. If you'll allow it, I want to do the same for you. I can only imagine how you'd feel around my cock."

One of us moaned. Maybe both. I could imagine all those things, and more. All those dreams I had when I was a kid—the sex in the shower, in the lockers, hell, even in an alley behind the school—scattered like leaves in a wind and were replaced by Charlie, who would now star in every fantasy I'd ever have.

He fumbled with the button on my pants. It wasn't easy with only one hand, but he was determined. I reached down to help, but he pushed me away.

"No, don't. I want to do this for you. Just sit back and enjoy, okay? Do that for me?"

A quick nod, and I leaned back. He touched me reverently. After he got my button undone, he unzipped my pants and pulled my cock out through the underwear fly. It wasn't warm in the cabin, despite the fire, and a chilly breeze wafted over my heated flesh. But all that went away when he wrapped his fingers around the shaft. I whimpered at the touch.

"Don't hold back, Matt. Come for me. I want to see you when it happens. There'll be plenty more in the future, if you'd like."

He stroked his hand up and down a few times, his touch featherlight, and I cried out his name as my head snapped back, my balls drew against my body, and several strong jets of warm come burst forth, splattering my abdomen and chest.

Charlie trailed his fingers through the mess, licked his index finger, smiled, and then said, "Wow. I was right. You *do* taste good."

I opened my eyes and he smiled.

"Thank you, Matt."

Still breathing hard, I asked, "For what?"

"Trusting me. Letting me touch you. Being mine."

The words were said with such sincerity, and it made me feel wanted like never before.

"Why don't you go ahead and take a shower? I'm sure you would rather not have that getting sticky in the hairs. Trust me, it's a bitch to get out."

"But what about you?" I asked, not really sure if I'd be able to go through with it.

"I'm fine," he promised. "This was for you. Go ahead and shower."

Slowly I stood, keeping my gaze locked on him. The smile on his face never wavered. I took a few hesitant steps, then stopped and turned around.

"No," I said, trying to inject as much authority into my voice as possible.

"No?" Charlie repeated.

"No," I said again. "You said this was for me, and I can't thank you enough, but… I want to do it to you too. Every time I helped you in the shower, I wondered what it would be like, and now that I'm so close, I'm not going to back away. Please, Charlie, I want—no, I *need*—to do this."

"Come here," he said, holding out his hand.

So much warmth came from it as I wrapped my fingers around his.

"My body is always yours to explore. I would love to have your hands on me, but don't want you to feel pressured. If it's what you want, then by all means, have at it." His cock pressed against his pants, tenting them almost obscenely. He let go of my fingers, lay back against the couch, and spread his legs.

I reached for him, then hesitated. Of course, he noticed.

"You don't have to do this," he reminded me.

I couldn't tear my gaze away from his groin. In my mind, memories flashed of the last time something like this happened. My breathing quickened, and I could feel my desire slipping away as I recalled the musky odor, the terror, and the pain.

"Matt, stop," Charlie said, keeping a gentle grip on my wrist. "There's no one here but us. Just you and me, like it should be. He's not here anymore. This is our home. Together. I love you, Matt."

He loves me. He loves me. He loves me.

"Yes, I love you. The color of your eyes, the softness of your hair, the blush of your skin. I love everything about you. We don't have to do anything at all. You had an experience already. We don't have to push it."

He loves me. He loves me. He loves me.

I collapsed onto the couch, curled into a ball. Charlie gently stroked my hair and continued to remind me of how much he loved me.

"I'm so sorry," I cried. "I want to, I do. I just...."

"Can't. And that's fine. Today you can't. Tomorrow might be another story. Every day brings new adventures, so don't worry about today, when tomorrow is around the corner."

He got up from the couch and began hobbling toward the bathroom. For some reason I pictured him walking out the door, and out of my life, all because I couldn't take care of his needs. My stomach clenched at the thought of being alone again. After having a taste of companionship, I didn't want to lose it.

"Where are you going?" I wailed. "Please don't leave me."

Charlie stopped in his tracks. "Whoa, hang on, sweetheart. Where is that coming from?"

I turned my gaze toward him, needing him to see my contrition. He had to believe how bad I felt. "I'm sorry. I'll try harder, I promise."

"Aw, fuck." He hurried back to the couch and dropped next to me. "Matt, I'm only going to get a towel to clean you up, I swear. I have no intention of leaving you." He stroked my cheek. "Until you tell me to go, you're stuck with me. Okay?"

I nodded, because the lump in my throat wouldn't allow me to speak.

"Two minutes, okay? Give me... well, okay, maybe five, because the bathroom is kinda far away and"—he tapped the cast on his leg—"I'm not as young as I used to be."

I laughed, but it turned into a sob. My emotions were all over the place. I'd had an orgasm from another person touching me, and I'd had the opportunity to return the favor. How would he look at me now?

As he promised, he came back a few minutes later with a warm cloth that he used to clean me up. I couldn't look at him, I was so ashamed. When he finished, he put the cloth into the basket, came back, and took my hand. "Come on," he said softly.

"Where are we going?"

He tugged my hand gently. "I'd like you to come with me. You'll need your jacket."

I picked up my coat from the hook at the door and slid into it. Charlie grabbed his and wrapped it around his shoulders. He opened the door, a cold wind blowing through it, then took me outside to the swing.

"Have a seat, please."

The tone of his voice had me wanting to run back to the house. He sounded defeated, angry.

"I'm so sorry," I whispered.

"Enough of that. Sit down, babe."

Warmth flooded me when he called me babe. It chased the creeping chill that had begun to permeate my body.

After I sat down, he took the seat next to me and held my hand. "First thing, I need you to know that I am not upset. At all. You told me no one had touched you before me. That orgasm had to be monumental. It was probably stressful for you. Why do you think I would be angry?"

I shrugged and turned away from him.

"No, we're not doing that. Look at me." When I didn't, he put a hand on my shoulder. "Matt? Please."

I turned and saw no censure in his expression. He smiled softly, then leaned forward and kissed me gently.

"You gave me a gift tonight. You let me touch you. Right now you're allowing me to hold you. How could I possibly be angry? Can I tell you something? It involves my ex, and if it would bother you, we don't have to talk about it."

My stomach cramped slightly, but I nodded. I had to trust him, because I loved him.

The realization struck me hard. I *loved* him. For the first time in my life, I was truly in love. Not a crush on Tommy Scolari, who looked amazing in his wrestling singlet. Not mooning over Alex Mulholland. Not wanting to go to the dance with Marty. But love. And I would do my damnedest to hold on to it.

CHAPTER FOURTEEN

"OKAY, WHERE to start…," Charlie said. "Mitch and I had been together for maybe six months. In retrospect, what I thought had been smooth sailing probably really wasn't. We argued quite often. Mitch liked stuff, and not the cheap kind of things either. He would fawn over something he saw, and I, like an idiot, would buy it for him. I thought that was what it meant to be in love."

Charlie wrapped an arm around me and pulled me close. I looked out at the yard. Heavy clouds covered the moon, but every so often, it would peek out and the ground would be alight in gleaming snowflakes. I sighed and sank into his warmth.

"We were never really compatible—I know that now. Mitch always expected to top, and I allowed it because I didn't mind bottoming at all. But once in a while, I thought it would be nice if we switched it up. I figured if he loved me as much as he claimed, we could at least try it. Mitch would be furious that I'd even think I could top him. I always backed down because it wasn't worth arguing about it. At least that's what I thought at the time.

"Anyway, I got it into my head that if I asked him to marry me, it would solve all of our problems and we'd find our happy ever after. When I came home and found him in bed with someone else, I realized that if I wanted to make a relationship work, it would have to be with someone who wanted the same things I did. Something we could both work toward. That man is you, Matt."

My head was spinning. I couldn't understand what this had to do with my failure to pleasure him as he had done me.

"I can see your confusion," he said, reaching up and stroking his fingers through my hair. "What I'm trying to say is, even if we never have sex, if all we can ever do is what we've already done, or even if we can't continue doing that, there is so much more between us than physical intimacy. Do you get what I'm trying to say?"

121

I thought I did, so I nodded.

"Good," he said, once again kissing my head. It was an affection I had grown to enjoy. "Sex is great, but it's not the be-all of life. Things like this—sitting on the porch, watching the moon, holding you—those are the important things I want to have every day. Everything else we do, no matter what it is, is simply frosting on the cake."

He laid it out for me. He didn't care about sex; he just wanted me. I could feel tears on my cheeks and cursed myself for it. For the past thirteen years, unless I woke from a nightmare, or got to the sad part in *My Side of the Mountain*, I rarely cried. Since meeting Charlie, it seemed to be a common occurrence.

"I wanna try again," I said, my voice scratchy.

"One day at a time, babe."

"No," I said as I shook my head. I knew if I didn't make the effort now, I might never be able to do it.

"Matt—"

"I said no." I slid away from him a bit so I could look him in the eye. "You don't know what it's like, living your life in fear. Haunted by the reminder of what's keeping you from experiencing things you've dreamed of. I do. Every day I'm reminded that I'm not, as my mother said, *normal*. I want the things other people experience. Love—both emotional and physical—family, making a life. I get what you're trying to tell me, but what you don't understand is that for me, that's only a half life. I need this, because without it, I'm going to always be afraid."

Charlie nodded. "Okay, how about this? We talk to your doctor, and if you decide you want to continue therapy, then we can look at it again?"

He was doing his best to give me an out, and I knew it, but I didn't want it. I had to prove to Charlie and to myself that I could do this.

"Come back in the house," I said, standing.

"Matt—"

"Now, please."

He didn't seem as enthused as I had hoped, but he did stand and allowed me to guide him back inside.

"Stand there for a minute," I told him, as I knelt and pulled down his pants and underwear. His cock hung limp, and when I gazed up at him, I only saw worry in his eyes.

"Matt, you don't need to prove anything. Please, let's just talk a while longer."

It wasn't easy to ignore his plaintive voice, but I did.

"Sit down," I said quietly.

Charlie sat and put a hand on my shoulder. I swallowed hard, reached out, and touched his dick with my fingertips. The warmth of it surprised me; I have no idea why. It began to puff up. It was longer and thicker than mine, with a flared head. I hadn't seen any but my own, but Charlie's was damned impressive. I wrapped my hand around it and gave a light squeeze, which caused Charlie to groan.

"You need to stop," he said but didn't try to move away.

His shaft began to harden, and I grinned to myself because it was me doing this to Charlie. I actually held him! And what's more, I enjoyed it.

Charlie's breathing began getting heavier, and I stroked harder. His head dropped back onto the couch and began to shake side to side. He started to whisper my name over and over, and that encouraged me to double my efforts. When his balls began to tighten up, I figured he might be close, but when he cried out my name and pushed up into my hand, I felt a rush of power and pride. His come coated his shirt, and he lay there, groaning.

"Did I do okay?" I asked, biting my lip.

"Can't talk. Dead now," he whimpered.

A laugh bubbled out of me. "I'm going to clean up."

He opened his eyes and pinned me with a stare. "Are you okay?"

I thought for a moment. "Yeah, I think so."

Three steps away, he called my name. I turned to him, and he grinned.

"In all the time I was with my ex, I never had an orgasm like that. Mitch liked getting off, then rolling over and going to sleep. You took care of my needs too. Thank you."

Charlie's ex was a selfish bastard. "You deserved better."

"I found it," he replied. "And I hope I never lose it."

Yeah, I didn't see that happening.

THE WEATHER stayed colder than the balls on a brass monkey. Charlie and I huddled inside as much as possible over the next two days. When he wasn't writing, we were curled up in front of the fire, sipping cocoa and sharing stories. He asked me about my childhood—which was awesome, how Clay was as a brother—I pleaded the fifth, then laughed about it, and for my most embarrassing moment—which was streaking through gym class, because the girls' volleyball team had set up for practice. In turn, I asked him how he got into writing.

"Before I started running, I was a chubby nerd. Comic books were my life, and I had the largest collection of anyone I knew. I thought it made me cool. Others had a different view on the whole thing. By the time I realized how bad it was, I was already ostracized. No one wanted to be friends with a geek, so I spent a lot of time alone. I began to write stories about my favorite heroes, only in my world, they were gay and had someone they loved with their whole heart. One day my mom found one of my stories—"

"Oh, shit."

Charlie grinned at me. "Yeah, that's what I thought too. When I walked in after school, she had me take a seat at the kitchen table with her and my father. She pulled out the yellow folder I used to write my stories in and showed me the stack of papers inside of it. I gotta tell you, I don't know if I ever sweated so hard. Everything in me was screaming to run away from home because they wouldn't understand. In the end I hemmed and hawed for several minutes as I tried to figure out a way out of the mess. Then she leaned over, cupped one cheek, and kissed me on the other. I sat there flabbergasted.

"She told me they'd read what I wrote and how proud of me they were. They said I had talent, and they wanted to help me with it. They bought me my first laptop, complete with writing software. I stared, waiting for the other shoe to drop, but it never did. We went out to dinner that night to celebrate. It was totally surreal."

"They didn't care you were gay?"

He laughed. "Nope. That was never even discussed. To them I was Charlie, and my happiness was the only thing that mattered. Oh, I got the safe sex lectures from Mom, and Dad warned me, whenever I got a boyfriend, he expected to meet him. Sadly the only one he met was Mitch. That… didn't go well. Mom said if I was happy, they would try to be happy for me, but they hated him. She said he seemed too smooth. Dad said he was insincere. Turned out they were both right. Wish I had listened."

My heart ached for Charlie. "I'm sorry things with him didn't work out." Then, though the thought pained me, I added, "Maybe you could—"

He held up a hand. "Oh God, no. Don't even think that I miss him. Leaving New York—leaving him—was the best thing I ever did. It brought me here and I got to meet you. I think that's a win right there."

I ducked my head as my cheeks heated.

"Don't blush yet. There's one more thing I need to talk to you about."

He sounded so serious, I began to fret.

"Stop that," he chided me. "What I wanted to say was that my parents would like to talk to you. I've told them that you're not comfortable around new people, but Mom is hoping that you'll allow her to talk to you on the phone."

I blinked a few times. "How does she know about me?"

Now it was Charlie's turn to blush. "I might have told her about you once or a few hundred times. Before the accident, you were a pretty popular topic of conversation. Mom said that she could tell from the sound of my voice I was in love. She told me I never sounded that way with Mitch and that she hoped to get to talk to you. There isn't any pressure, though. If you don't think you can do it, I'll explain it to her. I promise she'll understand."

He didn't say anything as I thought it through. Talking on the phone usually wasn't too bad. I talked often enough with Clay, and even though I was nervous when I spoke with him or Mr. Gianetti, it was easier than face-to-face. "Okay. Sure."

He seemed so surprised. "Really? Thank you!"

"When did you want me to do it?"

He glanced at the clock on the wall. "If you're up to it, we can try today. But if you need time to think about it, then we can revisit the idea in a week or two."

Charlie always seemed to put my needs first. He'd taken to going through the house daily to ensure things he'd used were put away—in the right places—or taking the scraps left over from the preparation of dinner and putting them into the compost heap that I used to enrich the soil for my plants. He did it all. Never once complained or made a fuss about why I had to do things in a certain way. He adapted to them instead. Having him here made my life easier, much to my surprise.

"Today would be good," I said, swallowing hard.

He ran his fingers through my hair. "Are you sure, Matt? She can wait, I promise."

"Yeah, I'll give it a try. Just… don't leave, okay?"

Visions of me freezing up ran through my head, and I could see Charlie's disappointed expression clear as a bell in my mind.

"Not going anywhere. Last chance. And before you answer, let me warn you… they're not like normal people. That might have a lot to do with how I turned out."

"You turned out just fine," I assured him. "I'm ready." I tried to keep my voice steady, even though my hands were shaking.

He pulled out his phone and dialed. He sat there, looking so pleased, and I curled up against him for the steadying contact.

"Hey, Mom. Good, thanks. How about you? Really? Excellent!" He pushed the mute button. "She went to the doctor for some tests, and he gave her a clean bill of health."

I smiled inwardly that he shared something so private with me. "Oh, awesome."

He let the button go and said, "Hey, Mom? I have someone here who would like to say hello. Just do me a favor—remember what we talked about. I don't want you scaring him away."

I heard the whoop in the background, as well as her calling for Alan, which I assumed was Charlie's father's name.

"Yeah, Mom? See, that right there is the kind of thing I'm talking about." Charlie gave me a look and rolled his eyes. "You're absolutely sure you want to subject yourself to this?" Charlie teased.

I heard his mother squawk indignantly, which made Charlie laugh.

"Mom, I'm going to give him the phone now. Please, I beg you, best behavior. Don't scare this one away."

"Hey!" I protested.

Charlie held the phone out to me. I wasn't surprised to find my palms sweating, my chest getting tighter, and my throat drying up like a desert.

"H-hello?" I croaked into the phone.

A soft sigh on the other end of the line. "You sound lovely," Charlie's mom gushed.

"Um. Thank you?"

Her laughter sounded like the song of some of my birds. I could imagine her standing outside with them, engaged in a duet to see which had the sweetest voice.

"So you're Matt? I'm so glad you felt safe enough to call."

"Can you… uh… hang on a second?" I asked, then hit the mute button before she could reply. I glared at Charlie. "What the hell did you tell her about me?"

He at least had the decency to flush. "I told her you lived alone because you were nervous around people, especially new ones. And, so you know, the only reason I talked to her was I needed her advice on how to woo you."

"Woo? No one says woo," I snapped. But secretly I was delighted that he had asked his mother.

"Woo is a nice word. My mom was the one who used it, so blame her. Do you want me to take the phone back?"

Did I? "No."

I let go of the mute button and tried to instill some confidence in my voice. "It's a pleasure to talk to you, Mrs. Carver."

"Oh, honey, no. You'll call me Gail. I much prefer that to Mrs. Carver." She paused. "Is that okay?"

"Thank you, Gail. That would be fine."

127

She, like her son, seemed to be too sweet for words. When she talked, I knew she was doing her best not to intimidate me, as her voice kept a soft, even tone. It should have bothered me, because I hated being treated differently, but knowing Charlie had talked to her in advance, told her about me? That made me smile.

"Charlie's dad would like to say hello. Is that okay?"

I took a deep breath, and she must have heard the hesitation.

"Honey, it's fine if you're not ready. He'll be happy to wait."

Well, damn. Now I knew where Charlie got his manners.

"I'd love to say hello," I lied. Really, there had been so many changes in the past week, I'd spent a lot of time touching my treasures. Charlie knew that during those times, it was best not to talk to me, at least until I found my center again. When he reached out and took my hand, my gaze met his.

"I love you," he mouthed.

"Hello!" a voice boomed over the phone. "Matt, right?"

"Yes, sir," I replied, cringing at the sound of his voice.

Charlie sighed and took the phone from my hand. "Dad. Too loud. Try about fifty decibels lower. He's not deaf."

Whatever his father was saying had Charlie grinning like a loon.

"More flies with honey is all I'm saying. Now, do you want to try again?" He turned his gaze to me, and I nodded. He smiled, and it helped calm the butterflies. "Okay, here you go."

"Hi, is this Matt?" he asked, his voice much softer than before.

"Yes, sir."

"Sorry. I get excited and tend to get loud. I don't want you to be afraid of me. I promise I don't bite."

"I'm not sure that's true" came a voice in the background.

"Shut up, Gail," he snapped, but I could hear the affection in his voice. "I am sorry. It's an honor to get to talk to you. Charlie hasn't stopped singing your praises. If it's to be believed, you could be the Second Coming."

My stomach flipped once more. I knew Charlie said he loved me, but to hear that he told his parents? God, that just about made everything perfect. And told me what I needed to do.

128

I didn't speak long with his parents. The more we talked, the more nervous I got. Charlie must have seen it, because he held out a hand to me, and I gave him the phone, then went around the room, grounding myself. After he hung up, he came up behind me and pulled me toward the couch. I sat down beside him, and he tucked me in to his side.

"They adore you," he whispered. "Mom thinks you're so sweet. Dad likes the fact that you're respectful. He didn't get much of that from Mitch, who thought it was cool to call him by his first name without even being asked to."

"I like them too," I said. "Your mom sounds wonderful. I really want...."

"Want what, baby?" he asked softly. "Tell me what you want."

"I want to go back to therapy." I was now more certain of this than I had ever been. Still, it scared me. What if they couldn't help me? What if it all got to be too much? Then I looked at Charlie and saw hope in his expression. "I never really thought about what I was missing out on until you came into my life. It's been me and these four walls for over a decade. I want to see what else is out there. I want to be able to stand up and hold out my hand to your parents and introduce myself properly. I want to be worthy of the words you said to your parents."

"You don't have to be anything other than Matt. People will like you and accept you for who you are, or they won't. Either way, the onus is on them. You should never have to change to satisfy anyone. I certainly hope you don't think I want you to be a different person for me."

"No," I replied. "I want to be a different person for me."

He kissed me on the head. "Then we'll do it. Together."

CHAPTER FIFTEEN

THE PHONE rang three times. I started chewing my nails, waiting for it to be answered. What could I say? It had been several years since we last spoke. Charlie told me I didn't have to do this, but he was wrong. I needed to clear the air if I wanted to move forward with my life.

"Hello?"

The voice sounded older. A lot wearier than I remembered. Nervousness gnawed at my stomach because I knew a lot of it had to do with me.

"Hi, Mom."

She gasped, and I heard her sob. I could picture her perfectly as she wrung her hands, and guilt welled up inside me. "Matt? Is it really you?"

"Yes'm," I whispered, the feelings of how I'd disappointed her, the sadness and pain almost crushing me. It was so easy to cut myself off, to pretend like it didn't matter, and then one small, insignificant thing brought it all rushing back.

"I—how are you?"

"I'm okay. How about you?"

She gave a rueful laugh. "I have a little bit of arthritis in my hands, but I'm still making pies for Christmas."

Every year my mother made pies and took them to Mr. Gianetti. He and his family, along with many others in the town, got together and did a food bank for those who weren't as fortunate. Back when I was a kid, too many people had to use it, because in a town like ours, jobs were hard to come by. I'd forgotten how important that was to her.

"I don't want to sound rude, but why are you calling? Not that you can't call," she hastened to add. "It's just... it's been a while."

She sounded so sad, and I didn't know how to make it better. I hadn't called to upset her, but that seemed to be the result. Charlie squeezed my hand, which helped me to focus. "I know what you and Clay did with Charlie."

130

Her voice broke when she spoke. "I know. Clay's devastated that he hurt you. And I'm so very sorry too. We just wanted you back. I know it was wrong of us, but—"

She had to stop. It wasn't her fault. None of this was. It never had been. One event from my past had left me vulnerable. Not weak, because Charlie was right. I wasn't weak at all. But my teacher had violated my trust, had made me push everyone else away, because I feared being hurt again.

"Mom, I want to go back to therapy," I interjected.

"You... do?" She sounded confused.

"Yes. I'm not sure how I feel about what you and Clay did, but... well, I fell in love with Charlie. I need him, but in order to be with him, I need to come to terms with who I am. In order to do that, I need to go back to see Dr. Rob."

She drew in a deep breath. "I knew you'd like Charlie. He seemed to be made for you."

The pictures I'd had of lean-bodied baseball players, whose posters covered my walls, gave away my preferences pretty easily.

"He's a writer," I told her, proud of that fact.

"I know. I read his books."

Charlie had told me she'd read his book, so that didn't surprise me. Much. But the thought of my mom reading some of the hot scenes had me scratching my head. "*You* read gay sex?"

She gave a snort. "I told you so many times, Matt, love is love. And even on paper, I could tell that Donald cares for Lucien very much. If you found a love like that, then I'm so happy for you."

I hadn't spoken to her for years. She should be angry. She probably would be right in hanging up on me for how I'd treated her. Instead she was telling me that she still loved me, and how happy she was that I'd found love. I could feel the burning in my eyes and knew the tears wouldn't be far behind. God, I'd become so emotional since I met Charlie. He must have seen, because he put an arm around my shoulder and pulled me close. I needed him, so I allowed it without complaint.

"I'm so sorry, Mom," I wailed. "I know you have to hate me, but—"

131

"You stop that!" she snapped. Then in a softer voice, she said, "You're my son. I could never hate you. I won't deny it hurt when you pulled away from us, but do you think I didn't understand? I know that my telling you I wanted you to be normal had to hurt you every bit as bad. Worse, because you were just a kid. I was supposed to be the adult, and I let my hurt feelings get the better of me. It was a cruel thing for me to say, and I regret it more than you'll ever know."

But I did know. I understood it better than she realized. I stewed in my hurt for years, and it festered. It became my mantra about why I was better off alone, because no one could hurt me then. I didn't need them to do it, though. I was hurting myself enough.

"Does Clay know?" Mom asked. "He was furious when he found out that Charlie was still out there with you."

I shook my head, even though she couldn't see me. "No," I answered. "I'll call him later. But I wanted to tell you that…. I wanted to say…." The lump in my throat made it so hard to get the words out. Even if she wasn't angry with me, I was upset with myself. I'd acted out and walked away from the only person who had ever given me anything without conditions. She deserved so much better than me for a son. "Mom, I love you."

"Oh, baby. I love you too. If you ever need me, I'm always going to be there for you."

"I'm going to try to get better," I sobbed, grateful when Charlie pulled me closer.

"You'll be how you think is best," she whispered. "I won't hurt you again by trying to turn you into someone you're not. We'll move forward at your pace, but I wouldn't object to a phone call every now and again."

"I will," I promised. "I should call Clay now. This could get ugly."

"It won't. He'll be thrilled, believe me. Your brother has always been your biggest supporter. He was the one who always kept an eye on you. I'll tell you a story, but you can't let him know I said so."

"Okay." I tried to sit up, but Charlie held me tight. His touch was warm, comforting, and I simply couldn't work up any annoyance at being pampered.

"After you moved, he came to me and worried about you being out there alone. His biggest fear was what would happen if you got hurt and there wasn't anyone to help you. So he took it upon himself to come up with contingencies and ways around them. Every time he knew you were out fishing, he'd come over and measure windows, doors, glass from your greenhouse. Any and everything he could think of, so if something ever happened, he'd always know how to fix it."

The realization struck me. When Charlie and Clay had come out to fix the door, I never once questioned how Clay had one that fit. I looked up at Charlie, who sat smiling down at me. "Did you know about my door?" Until that very moment, I had never even thought about why Clay would just happen to have a door he could put up at my house.

He smiled. "I asked him the next day. He fessed up to me about what he'd done, and even though I thought it was sneaky, I was really damn glad he'd thought of it. You don't know how much your brother loves you."

It was beginning to look like I was the only one who didn't. Mom knew. Charlie knew.

"Was that Charlie?" Mom asked.

"Yes'm."

"Can I speak to him for a moment? You're welcome to put me on speaker so you can hear too."

I fumbled with the phone briefly, then pressed the button. "Okay, you're on speaker."

"Hi, Charlie."

"Hi, Mrs. Bowers."

She was quiet for a moment. "Thank you for being there for my son," she said, her voice choked with emotion. "He needed you, and I'm glad you stayed."

"Oh no," Charlie said. "I needed him more than he ever needed me. Until I met Matt, I hadn't written much on Donald's next book. I lost my direction, but Matt became my muse. When I'm with him, the words flow so smoothly, because I found the one thing I was missing. I found love again."

I tossed the phone onto his lap and pushed out of his grip before I ran for the bedroom and buried my face in the pillow.

Charlie came hobbling in a few moments later. "A little overwhelmed?"

When I didn't reply, he sat next to me and stroked my hair. It had become something I'd woven into my needs. His touch had become one of those things I needed in my life to make it right. He'd become an integral part of who I was. Or maybe who I wanted to become.

"I know I say this a lot, but you have to give yourself time. You've taken a lot of steps in a short time, and it's bound to play havoc with your nerves. Slow your pace. Take a month, a year—hell, a decade. Whatever feels comfortable. I'll be by your side, holding your hand. This is it for me, Matt. I'm in this for the long haul. If we never leave this property again, I'm okay with that."

"I know." I sniffled. "I understand what you're saying, but I want to go see my mom. To sit on the sofa and have tea with her while we talk about Christmas. To see Clay shaking his gifts and asking me not to tell Mom I caught him." I looked up at him, pleading with my eyes for him to understand. "I want my life back."

He urged me down onto the bed and covered me with the comforter. "You need to rest now. Tomorrow is a whole new day, and we're going to start it fresh."

"But I'm not sleepy," I whined. Truth be told, Charlie was right. I was beyond exhausted.

He leaned over and kissed my forehead, then ruffled my hair. "Want me to read you a bedtime story? I think I owe you one."

I pulled the covers up to my chin, then gave him a grin. "Yes, please."

"What would you like to hear?" he asked, no teasing at all in his tone.

How had I gotten so lucky?

"Would you read *My Side of the Mountain*?"

"Oh, I love that book! When I was little and we were living in New York, I wanted to run away to the woods and live far from any people. Maybe that's why I'm so comfortable here. It's my dream come true."

"Except I'm here," I said, trying to tease him a little.

He smiled at me. "That's what makes it a dream. Now close your eyes. I'll be back in a few."

After he left, I snuggled in deeper. I heard him in the kitchen, and when I called out to ask what he was doing, he simply said he'd be in shortly. A few minutes later, I could hear the thump of his crutch as he crossed the floor, and then he appeared at the door, with two mugs in his hand and the book tucked under his arm.

"I made us some hot cocoa," he said, placing the mugs on the nightstand. He went around to the other side of the bed and lay atop it. I handed him his cup, and he put it aside. He opened the book and began to read. It was totally different from when I read the book myself. Charlie's voice was deep and his dulcet tones made hearing the story a whole new experience. The problem was, I fell asleep before he reached the third page.

CHARLIE WAS still sleeping when I woke up at five. The book was open on his chest, and some of the pages had fluttered to the floor. I picked them up and bound them with the rubber band again. I looked at Charlie, his face so placid. My heart thumped a little harder when I remembered his words of love. I wanted to wake him, ask him to say them again, but he needed his rest, so I left him in the bedroom while I went to start the coffee.

As the machine bubbled away, I pulled out my phone and scrolled through the contacts until I found Clay. I dialed his number and waited for him to answer. After four rings, I started to wonder if he was going to ignore my call.

"Bowers," he groaned into the phone. "This better be good, because I have a gun and I'm not afraid to use it."

"Did I wake you?"

"Matt?" he asked, his voice a lot more alert.

"Hey. I'm sorry if I disturbed you."

"No, it's fine. Late night. One of the guys called out, so I pulled an extra shift. Just got to bed an hour or so ago."

"Oh. I can call back later."

"Don't hang up," he pleaded. "Please. I'm sorry, Matt. I had no business acting the way I did."

"No, you didn't. But I understand. Can I ask you a question?"

"Ask me anything you want."

I poured the first cup of coffee, the rich aroma filling my nose. I leaned up against the counter, mug in hand, trying to think of the best way to phrase what was going through my head. "Do you love me?"

He snorted. "That's a stupid question, and I think you know it. You're my brother—how could I not?"

"It's easy, believe me."

I heard him shuffling around on the other end. "Yes, I love you. Is that the only reason you called?"

The coffee was smooth and warmed my insides as I took a sip. "No. I... I need to talk to you. Can you come over today?"

He didn't say anything for a few moments. "Seriously?"

"Yes. We need to talk."

"Okay, yes. I can leave now if you're staying up."

Charlie was still sleeping, but I figured it was fine. "When you wake up."

"Trust me, I won't be able to go back to sleep now. I'm awake. I'll be there within the hour."

"Okay." Then I figured I'd best break the news to him while he was on the phone, just in case he changed his mind. I didn't want him and Charlie getting into a fight. "Charlie's here."

He took a quick intake of breath. "Are you okay with that?"

"Yes. I... I need him. I know it won't make any sense to you, but—"

"He's part of your world? I get it. Why do you think I told him he had to go slow? You needed to accept him as someone you were seeing every day so he'd be ingrained in your mind. I remember all the things that happened when we were kids and either Mom or I would bring something new into the house. I watched your reactions and did my best to make things easy on you. I do pay attention, you know."

Sneaky shit. Rat bastard full of love for his brother who had been nothing but trouble.

"I know I don't say it often enough…. Okay, I haven't said it for years, but I love you, Clay. Thank you for being my big brother."

"But I'm not—"

"I'm older, but you're the one who went out of his way to make my life better. So you're a lot more mature than me. Well, except for that gun comment. That was pretty juvenile."

He chuckled, and a weight lifted from my shoulders. Maybe we'd be okay after all. "I'll see you soon, Matt."

He disconnected, and I stared at the phone for a few moments, then slid it back into my pocket.

"Clay?" came Charlie's voice.

I nodded, too choked with emotion to actually speak. The familiar *step-thump* of his gait had me smiling, and I sighed when his arm wrapped around my waist, happy for the fact he understood my need to have a connection right now.

"I'm proud of you. I hope you know that."

That made one of us. All I saw myself doing was correcting my own lifetime of mistakes.

"Turn around," he said, in a tone that told me he understood my feelings.

I spun and buried my face in his neck. He backed us up to the couch and sat down, holding me against him.

"I'm here to talk if you need me, you know. You don't have to, but I wanted to make sure you knew the offer was on the table."

Every time Charlie held me, I felt safer than I had in so long. He had this aura about him that told me he cared and would do his best not to hurt me. It dawned on me that I needed that if I was ever going to heal.

"I asked Clay to come over because I want to talk to him about things. But I need you to know that no matter what else, if I have to choose between him and you, I'm going to take you every time."

Charlie sat back. "Hold on now. I need you to listen to me, okay? Don't say anything, just hear what I'm telling you. You never want to be forced to choose one person over another. It's not fair, and in the end, you'll end up regretting it. Clay and I are adults, and we'll handle our problems like it, I promise. I would never ask, or want, you to feel you needed to split from your family for me."

My laugh bordered on hysterical. "I split from them a long time ago."

He stroked my cheek, and his gaze bored into me. "True, but that was your own choice. It wasn't about me. I don't want you to do this because of me. I only want you to do it if you think there is no other way. Remember, Clay has always been there for you. He came when you called and didn't hold it against you that you've pushed him away. You're his brother, and he loves you. Let him do that now."

Charlie was too good to be real. No one could be this patient and caring. "How are you so perfect?"

That got a belly laugh out of him. "Oh, I am *so* not perfect. You know how you are about your stuff? I'm the same way with my writing. I hate it when a story isn't going like I want. I'll fuss and fume about it, cuss to myself. Hell, I'll even yell at the characters if they're not behaving like they're supposed to. So not perfect, and I would appreciate it if you don't put me on a pedestal, because it gives me that much further to fall."

Okay, fine. Maybe he wasn't perfect in every way, but in my eyes, he was as close as any person I'd ever met.

CHAPTER SIXTEEN

THE KNOCK on the door had my nerves jangled. For the last hour, I had told myself I was ready to face Clay, but in truth, I wasn't. I believed he loved me, and I hoped that extended to him wanting what I thought was best for me.

"He's here," I said, stating the obvious.

Without comment Charlie stepped over to the hearth and poked at the fire he'd started to ward off the chill that permeated the house.

I'd been sitting and worrying about how things were going to go. Things had gotten marginally better when Charlie sat next to me, wrapped his arm around my shoulder, and told me he was proud of me. For a few moments before Clay arrived, I felt calm and steady.

Now? I was so nervous I was shaking.

"Want me to get it?" Charlie asked.

I shook my head, took a deep breath, and straightened my spine. I could do this. I *would* do this.

As soon as the door opened, a gust of bitterly cold air swirled in the doorway, bringing a light dusting of snow with it. Clay stood on the porch, bundled in his flannel jacket, gray woolen cap, and black snow pants.

"Please tell me you have coffee," he begged as he stumbled dramatically through the door. I looked for Charlie, wanting to hold his hand, but saw him coming back from the kitchen.

"Decaf," Charlie replied as he handed Clay a cup.

"Don't care. It's hot, and that's good enough for me."

I breathed a sigh of relief that they hadn't jumped right back to the threats of violence. Maybe it was a good sign.

"Do you want to sit?" I asked Clay.

"Sure, that would be nice." He stepped toward the couch, then stopped to remove his snowy jacket and boots. He grinned at me. "I can be civilized, you know." Then he hurried over and stretched out in front of the fire. "God, that feels good. I don't know how you can stand it up here. It's like thirty degrees colder than in town."

I ignored what I thought was a subtle dig, but Charlie didn't.

"It's warmer here than in town because this place has so much heart."

Clay held up his hand. "I'm not trying to be a dick. I'm serious. It's warmer in town, but this place is cozy."

"Sorry," Charlie murmured, taking my hand in his.

"No, you have absolutely no reason to be sorry. I do, though." He swallowed, getting a pained expression on his face. "I almost lost my brother because I wasn't willing to accept he could be happy living the way he was. I'm not going to say I agree with it, but it wasn't my decision to make. I had no business trying to force him to change who he is."

"But, Clay, I—"

"Please, let me finish."

Charlie sat on the opposite end of the couch and pulled me closer. I had the insane desire to be on his lap, with his arms wrapped around me, but the casts wouldn't come off for another week. Instead I sat on the arm of the couch and gave Clay my undivided attention.

"I was selfish," he continued, his gaze locked on mine. "I wanted Matt to be there for Sunday dinners so we could talk about things. I wanted to tell him about the girl I was dating. The changes on Main Street. I wanted us to sit in our pajamas around the Christmas tree with Mom, drinking coffee at four in the morning because I was too excited to sleep. Did you know I have every gift I bought for you still wrapped in a closet at home?" He coughed when he tried to chuckle. "I bought you a Nirvana shirt the year after you moved out. I saw it when I was out on a date and had to get it. Then I realized you wouldn't see it, and I had no idea what to do to make things right."

I could see tears on his cheeks now, and my heart stuttered.

"Mom told me you know about me being out here when you were gone. I'm sorry, but it was the only way I could connect with you. I swear I wasn't stalking you.... Well, okay, not much. But goddammit, Matt. I missed you so fucking bad, it tore me up inside. You don't know what it's like, knowing your brother is less than an hour away and you can't just drop by to see him."

I stood, wanting to launch myself at him, but Charlie kept his grip on my hand. When I glanced at him, he gave a small shake of his head.

"Did you ever once think about us? When it was Christmas, did you wonder what we were doing? How we were getting along? Shit, you didn't even *call* on the holidays. Mom and I stopped decorating because there didn't seem to be any sense in it. Our lives stopped when you left. It was like you fucking *died*," he shouted. "No, it's worse than that, because if you were dead, we'd at least be able to mourn you."

His eyes went wide, and his cheeks were stained red. "I'm sorry, I didn't mean that. Oh, fuck, Matt. I am so very sorry." All the anguish burst out of him, and he threw himself at me and wrapped me in his arms. I was uncomfortable, but I allowed him to hold me. "We were lost without you," he whispered in my ear. "We still are."

Charlie let go of my hand, and I patted Clay on the back. We stood there, him embracing me, for a few more moments before he stepped back. His eyes were red, and he looked exhausted.

"You built this perfect world for yourself here but took away the one thing that made ours right. Do you understand that?"

I nodded. I did understand it, but I'd convinced myself I would never get better, so I stopped trying. What was the sense? Looking at Clay now, how could I not realize what I'd done?

"You weren't the only one who was selfish," I told him. "I thought my life was over and I'd never get it back. I ran away from my problems, instead of trying to face them. I'm sorry for what I did to you and Mom. I know I'll never be able to make up for the hurt I caused you both."

He gave me a sad smile. "And I'm sorry for trying to force you to change. Be who you are, Matt. If you're happy, then I'll do my best to be happy for you." He turned to Charlie. "As for you, I was an asshole. I asked for your help and then didn't like the results. I didn't even look to see how happy Matt was. I'll be honest, I don't think he's smiled much since he left. When I look at him now, though? You helped him. At least he's coming to terms with himself."

"I am. That's part of what I wanted to talk to you about," I said. A quick breath, a glance at Charlie, and I told him why I'd wanted him to come over. "I'm going to go back to therapy."

Clay blinked a few times. "Seriously? Please don't tease me about this."

"No teasing," I promised. "And I have you to thank for it."

He seemed rattled. "Me?"

"You sent me Charlie. He made me want things, like a life outside of these four walls. Oh, I don't intend on moving. Charlie's going to live here with me, but I want my family back. Do you think you can accept him?"

"Yes!" Clay shouted. Then he ducked his head. "Yes, definitely. Like I said, what happened was my fault, and I'm very sorry about it."

Charlie held out his hand, but Clay surprised me when he pulled him into a firm but gentle hug.

"You're a good man, Charlie Brown," Clay said, then snorted.

Much of the tension I was feeling dissipated immediately. While they talked, I went around and touched my treasures again to remind myself that things were good and hopefully would get better from here on out.

CHAPTER SEVENTEEN

One Year Later

"SO, MATT, how are things with Charlie?"

Things were beyond wonderful. A combination of medication, exercise—I was now running with Charlie every day—and coping techniques had allowed me to take my first trip with him. We didn't go far, but it was one of the most important steps in my life. We packed an overnight bag and checked into a motel on the outskirts of town. That night we went to dinner to celebrate Charlie's new book contract with my mom, Clay, and Trish, his girlfriend of the last six months. She was a delight, and Clay was lucky to have her in his life, because she took absolutely zero bullshit from him.

We celebrated as a family for the first time since I'd pretty much run away from my problems. Even though Christmas wasn't for several months yet, Clay brought everything he'd saved up for me. He took great joy in handing me all of the gifts I'd missed out on. I cried at nearly every one of them, especially the Nirvana shirt, which I clutched to my chest.

It was hard to believe how much my life had changed. I found myself needing to touch my items less, and I didn't freak out when they weren't in my perfect order. Oh, I still had my moments. Like the day Charlie forgot to put the cap back on the toothpaste and it sent me into a tailspin. But where before I would have to run around the house, touching all my things to ground myself, I stood in the bathroom and did the visualization techniques Dr. Rob had taught me. Those were usually enough to stave off the panic.

"They're good. No, better than. His new book comes out next week, but he's bringing me a copy home today!"

Dr. Rob chuckled. "You like those books, do you?"

"God, yes. I've been waiting on this one for so long. When he told me they'd picked it up, I started badgering him about when I'd be able to read it. His plane is landing at three, so he should be home about six or so."

"Then we'll see what we can do about keeping this appointment short. I wouldn't want to deprive you of your reading."

I let my gaze wander over his desk. Dr. Rob had never been a messy man, but his desk wasn't very tidy. The penholder sat in the middle of his desk, and I simply stared at it. There was a small desire to move it, but today I was able to keep my hands to myself. Of course, he noticed.

"Do you want to move it?"

I thought about it for a few moments. "No," I replied. "It seems fine where it is. Though you might want to consider dusting it."

He laughed. "You've come a long way, Matt." He glanced at his watch. "I think that's enough for today. You have a book to get home to."

As I stood, I took a look at Dr. Rob. He'd aged but was still a handsome man. He had a warm manner that drew me in and made me feel comfortable. Again, something I had forgotten in my desire to get away from everyone and everything.

"Dr. Rob?"

"Yes, Matt?"

"Thank you."

He tipped his glasses a little, showing off his light blue eyes. "For what?"

"Not giving up on me, I guess. Clay told me you were asking after me."

He folded his hands on the desk. "When you came to me, I believed together we could help make things better for you. When you stopped coming, it niggled at my mind, made me wonder what I could have done differently. But, to tell the truth, you've done very well for yourself. And I think together we are going to make even greater strides."

My cheeks warmed a little. Dr. Rob walked around the desk and held out his hand. I took it, then pulled him in for a brief hug. He stepped back, seemingly surprised.

"Merry Christmas, Dr. Rob," I said, then made my way out of the door and onto the chilly street. The avenue was lined with Christmas decorations. Each store had them up as well. I'd forgotten how much I loved the holiday. After I checked the time, I realized I could make a last-minute decision to stop in to see Mr. Gianetti. He hugged me like a long-lost son. Instead of the flare of panic I usually felt, I sank into the warmth.

"Matthew!" he said, patting me on the back. "It's so good to see you. How's Charlie?"

"He's good, thank you. How are you and the missus?"

He waved a dismissive hand. "She thinks I need to lose weight," he scoffed as he patted his well-rounded belly. "I told her I can still fit into the pants I wore when I was eighteen."

I laughed. "She knew it was a lie, right?"

He sighed and his lower lip jutted out. "She took away my cheesecake. What kind of wife takes away a man's cheesecake, Matty?"

"One who loves you and wants to keep you around," I answered.

"Do you have plans for the holiday?" he asked, ignoring my comment.

"I'm helping Mom bake pies for the shelter," I answered, a bit of pride shining through.

"Really? Excellent! I hope you and your guy will stop by if you're able."

We intended on it. Charlie fussed over whether or not I thought I was ready. It would be the biggest event I'd been to, and he worried it might be too much, too soon. And it might be, but it was a chance I was willing to take. For the first time in so many years, I could see choices stretched out in front of me, just waiting for me to take one.

After we finished talking, I did a little shopping, picking up some things for dinner. It still amazed me that I was able to do this, and I wondered what my life would have been like if I hadn't given up on therapy to move out to the woods. But, as Dr. Rob told me, I couldn't dwell on the past. I had to look to the future Charlie and I were building.

I caught a cab back to our place, trying to decide if I should renew my license to save on the not-too-cheap fees I was paying to have them come get me and take me back.

When I got home that night, Charlie wasn't there yet. He'd taken a day trip to New York to visit with his publisher, who wanted to talk to him about the book tour they were planning on doing. Though we hadn't discussed it, I wanted to attend with him, for moral support if nothing else.

I texted him to let him know I was home. He immediately replied, saying he would be home within the hour, and he had my copy of the book with him. I was so excited I could barely contain myself. He kept saying this book was going to be a game changer, and I would be the first person, outside of his publishing company, who would get to see what it was.

I made beef goulash for dinner, something rich and hearty to combat the pervasive chill that seemed to have settled on our land. As I glanced out the window, I saw the approaching lights, and my heart began to beat faster. Charlie got out of his truck and strode toward the house, my book in his hand. I rushed for the door, threw it open, and reached out.

"Did you miss—"

I snatched my copy of *Comes a Foul Wind* from his grip. "Dinner is on the stove. Help yourself," I murmured as I rushed for the couch.

He chuckled. As he passed by where I sat, he bent over and kissed my head. "Missed you too, babe."

The story gripped me from the first page. Tremaine could best be described as an antihero, because he did a lot of things no good person would do. When I'd tried to explain my fascination with the world to Clay, he kept telling me how Donald would probably be arrested for some of the stunts he pulled. Of course, he had to get a copy of the book to find out what I was talking about, and now he was hooked too. He did say he skipped the sex scenes, though.

"So what do you think so far?" Charlie asked, taking a seat beside me.

I glanced up. I'd been there for over two hours. "Fuck, this is good," I muttered, not wanting to stop reading.

"It's time for bed, you know."

"One more chapter, okay? Please?"

He glanced over to see where I was and smiled. "Sure. I'm going to nap here, if that's okay. Long trip, but I didn't want to be gone overnight."

The thought touched my heart. "Glad you came back."

"Oh, I'm always going to come back. At least as long as you're here," he said, his voice filled with sleep. A moment later, he was snoring.

I knew I should put the book down, but goddammit, I'd waited almost a year for this to come out. I promised myself one more chapter and then I'd take Charlie to bed. Maybe tonight we'd exchange hand jobs again. Or maybe we'd go a little bit farther. We hadn't done anything beyond that, as much as I wanted to. Charlie insisted we were going to take it slow, and I appreciated that fact. Being able to touch him was good enough for me.

The end of the chapter was drawing near, and I'd only finished about half the book. But a promise was a promise. Things took an odd turn when Lucien got arrested for murder, as the police found the body he said he'd seen. Tremaine strode into the police station, larger than life. They took him to see Lucien, who sat seemingly completely unbothered by the events around him.

"Aren't you going to ask if I did it?" Lucien asked, his voice silky smooth. He studied his nails, then buffed them against his shirt before he turned his gaze back on his lover.

"Why? Should I?" Tremaine fired back. "Is that what you want? Me to ask if you're a killer?"

Lucien snorted. "Why not? Everyone else is wondering."

"I never wonder about you, Lucien. You are the one solid thing in my whole life, and I never doubt that. I do have a question I need answered, though."

"I figured you might" came the cold reply.

Tremaine fished a hand into his pocket and withdrew a small pewter gray box. He held it out and popped the top open. Inside was a brushed metal band with gold edging on the top and bottom. "Do you think you might wanna marry me?"

"Oh my God!" I squealed, jolting Charlie from his sleep.

He lurched up. "What? What's wrong?"

I reached over and grabbed him by the hand. "Tremaine asked Lucien to marry him!"

"Well, yeah," Charlie replied, yawning. "I told you it would happen eventually."

"But in a jail?" I demanded, completely incredulous as to how Charlie had written it.

Charlie grinned. "Okay, it's not the most romantic setting, I admit."

When he'd said that Tremaine would propose, I'd expected something a little more... I don't know. Hearts and flowers? Not in jail when his lover was the prime suspect in a murder case.

"So you're done reading for the night? Because I'm very tired."

"But... but...."

"Are you upset because it wasn't a really sweet gesture? Could you really see Tremaine getting down on one knee and asking Lucien to spend their lives together?"

Well, no. Now that he said it that way, it would have seemed weird. "No, I guess not."

"He's not really one for over-the-top declarations," Charlie reminded me. "Me, on the other hand...." Charlie slipped a hand into his pocket and withdrew a pewter gray box. He opened the lid, and inside was a brushed metal band with gold edging on the top and bottom. My shoulders started shaking as he got down on one knee. "Do me a favor, would you? Read the dedication to the book."

I flipped back to the beginning and started to read.

This book is for Matt, the love of my life, who brings me joy that I couldn't find anywhere but in his arms. If he's reading this, I need him to answer a question for me. Do you think you might wanna marry me?

I began to cry. I looked up at Charlie, who had gone blurry around the edges. "Really?" I squeaked.

"You're the only thing in my life I need to keep," he said, his voice husky. "Life just makes more sense when you're in it. So what do you say?"

Married? Me? I had honestly never considered it before, even with Charlie here.

"You're not saying anything," Charlie said quietly. "If you don't feel ready—"

"Yes."

"Yes… what?"

I cupped his cheeks in my hands and pulled him toward me. "Yes, I'll marry you."

He chuckled. "I love you, and tonight I'd like to show you how much."

Did he mean…. *Oh hell.*

CHAPTER EIGHTEEN

WE WENT into the bathroom together, and I was grateful for the fact that our shower was big enough for two of us.

"I've been traveling all day," he explained. "After I met with the publisher, I went and saw my parents and Teresa. They all said hi. Had to help Dad shovel, so I'm sweaty and probably not very fresh. I want to make sure we don't have any issues." He grabbed the washcloth and liquid soap, which smelled of cedar and mint. He applied a dab and began running it over my chest. "You don't know how much I love your body," he whispered. "The fact that I get to touch you like this turns me on so much. Knowing no one else ever has, or ever will, makes it that much better."

He treated me gently, as though I was made of spun glass and might shatter at a touch.

"If this gets to be too much, you have to tell me, okay?"

I nodded.

"No, I need to hear your voice. I have to know this is all right. I won't continue if it worries you or makes you nervous."

"It makes my stomach quiver when you touch me," I admitted. "But I'm not afraid."

"Good. I'm glad."

Soft, sure strokes across my body had me achingly hard. Whenever Charlie touched me as we shared an intimate moment, I thanked God or whoever wanted to take credit for it. They really knew their stuff when they designed nipples, because mine... oh hell, yes.

When Charlie handed me the cloth, I didn't hesitate to begin exploring his body. I moved down, until I had to kneel in front of him to reach his legs. Before this, I had never really had his dick in my face. It hung heavy and hard, and begged to be touched. I reached up and stroked it with my hand. When he shuddered, I grinned.

"Have I ever told you what it's like touching you?"

His expression told me he wanted to know. "Not that I recall."

"Your body is firm from the running, but it's so soft beneath my fingers. It intrigues me the way your muscles flex as I stroke them. And I find it amazing the way your cock seems to be attached to every nerve ending I touch and jumps when I do."

"What can I say? My body appreciates your hands. And it looks forward to getting to know you better."

Charlie stared into my eyes, and his loving gaze overwhelmed me. He reached for me and put his hands under my arms to pull me up. I got a smile, so sweet and gentle, before Charlie leaned in and kissed me. When his tongue touched my lips, I opened for him. He swept into my mouth, his tongue teasing mine, coaxing it to play. When I took the invitation, my heart soared. Charlie threw his arms around me and cupped the back of my head, drawing the kiss deeper. He stepped back and gazed into my eyes once more.

"I love you."

"I love you too," I whispered.

He took my hand as we stepped out of the shower. We each took a towel and dried ourselves off. After, he put an arm around my waist and led me to the bedroom. My stomach flipped as I thought about what we might be getting ready to do. When he pulled out his phone, I was surprised. I hadn't expected that at all.

"You're going to take pictures?"

He laughed. "No, but maybe later. We could have someone post it online for us, and we'll act all surprised. But that's not what this is for." He opened a file and held his phone out to me.

"What's this?" I asked as I studied the screen.

"My test results. I want you to know I'm clean. I haven't had sex with anyone since I walked out on Mitch, and even when we were together, we always used condoms."

What he was saying didn't make any sense to me at first. Then it dawned on me what he meant. "You want to…?"

"Only if… when you're comfortable with it," he rushed to explain. "I just wanted you to know the option is open."

The thought of sex with Charlie had been on my mind for the longest time, but to go without a condom? Even I'd heard the stats growing up, and though I knew there were drugs out there, none of them was a cure.

"I don't know. I've never had anyone… you know."

He gave me a Cheshire grin. "That's why I want you to do me."

I took a step back. "You what?"

He came closer and took my hand. "I, Charlie Carver, want you, Matthew Bowers, inside me." He looked down and grinned at my cock jutting out in front of me. "It seems like that idea appeals to you."

Yes, it did. So very, very much. "But I don't know what to do," I admitted.

"Then I'll teach you. Come on."

He guided me to the bed. My erection had flagged because the thought that Charlie wanted me to…. God, almost thirty, and I still couldn't think it.

"Hey, remember, no pressure. If you're not ready, then we wait."

This man… *my fiancé*… had been by my side for over a year. I'd known him even longer. Beyond our one problem, he'd never given me another reason to doubt he loved me and would never hurt me.

"Show me," I said softly.

He lay back and pulled me down to him. Every move was gentle, but the hesitation was gone. He trusted me to know my mind.

"First, we relax both of us," he said, bringing our lips together. Soft kisses, sweet, warm. God, I loved kissing him. I'd never kissed anyone else, but I doubted they'd have his sweet and tangy flavor. I clung to him as we continued the kisses, and when he stroked my skin, I moaned into his mouth.

He pulled back and looked me in the eye. "You like that, huh?" he teased.

Instead of answering, I went in for another kiss. This time he hummed.

"Touch me, Matt. Please."

I slid my hands over his chest, rubbing over his nipples, which perked up under my touch.

"I like it when you do that," he said, his voice huskier than I'd ever heard it. "If you wanted to pinch them lightly, that would be awesome."

Deciding to take him at his word, I gave them a light tug. He groaned, and it was the most sensuous thing I'd ever heard. I spent a little more time on his chest, until his nipples were red and puffy. When I moved my hand again, he whimpered.

"You're so good at that. You made it feel damn good."

I knew he was critiquing my performance and his words were meant to put me at ease. Thankfully, they did. I slid my hand down and wrapped my fingers around his shaft.

He grabbed my wrist and stopped me. "No, don't do that. I've been looking forward to being with you for so long, and it won't take much to bring me to orgasm. What I want to do now is show you how to prepare me. Okay?"

I nodded, then replied, "Yes, okay."

He reached over to the nightstand and pulled out the bottle of lubricant that Mr. Gianetti had sent along last year. He broke open the seal on it, which sent a shiver coursing through me. After popping the top, he put a small bit on his fingers and rubbed them together.

"With lube, a little goes a long way. It doesn't normally take a lot to get someone ready. It's more about patience and learning to read your partner. I'm going to show you what you do."

He reached between his legs and slowly rubbed his fingertip over his hole, which twitched each time he did. He groaned as he sank the finger in just up to the first knuckle. "God, it's been so long, I forgot how good this feels," he said, pressing in a little more.

I watched, fascinated, as his finger disappeared, then reappeared. He repeated the movement several times, his moaning enough to bring me back to rock hardness.

"After your partner is comfortable with one finger, you should move to add another," Charlie said. "It usually takes two or three before they loosen up enough to take you." He glanced down at me. "In your case, I'm thinking three," he said, gracing me with a smile. He reached for the lube again, but I stopped him.

"Can I?"

"If you're sure, yeah, go for it."

He lay back against the pillow and drew his knees up. I grabbed the bottle and did what Charlie had. Except I ended up with a lot more lube.

"It's fine," he told me, reaching down and grabbing one of the towels from the bathroom. He handed it to me, and I wiped my hand off, doing my best to focus on Charlie and not the fact the towels didn't belong on the floor. "Try again."

This time I squeezed lightly and got a few drops instead of a small stream.

"You're going to want to go slow to start. There's a slight burn when you first enter, but it quickly becomes something amazing."

I moved my hand down between his legs. When my fingers touched his hole, it quivered, and I drew back.

"Did I hurt you?" I asked, praying I hadn't.

"No," he said, a wide smile on his face. "You're doing just fine. Try again."

This time my fingers breached him, and he hissed. I watched his expression. He wasn't in pain, I knew that, so I didn't stop. I did as he had and pushed in slightly.

"Oh God," he groaned. "Go deeper."

I pressed in until my fingers were buried to the second knuckle. He let me explore, moving my fingers in different ways to see if it heightened his pleasure at all. Before I realized it, my fingers were all the way inside of him.

"Do you feel that bump?" he asked. "That's my prostate. If you touch it lightly, it feels so goddamn good."

I searched for it, and when I brushed against it, Charlie groaned.

"Fuck yes!" he cried, his hips pushing off the bed. "Add another finger now."

There was no hesitation this time. Seeing the look of rapture on his face had me willing to do anything he wanted. I quickly spread a little more lube and slowly pressed the fingers into his opening. Watching them sink in was fascinating. He let me go at my own pace, but I noticed his head rocking back and forth as his hips canted.

"Matt, I need you now. Do you think you're ready?" he asked, his voice pleading.

"I…. Maybe?"

He opened his eyes. "Baby, it's okay if you're not. I swear, I won't be upset or angry. I think what you did today is amazing."

"No, I want to, but…. Would you be hurt if I used the condom?"

He chuckled as he sat up and stroked my arm. "No, not at all. I only showed you the report so you knew. If we decide one day to go bareback, then we do. It's not a deal breaker, I promise."

My hands trembled slightly as I reached for the box of condoms Mr. Gianetti had sent me long ago. I pulled one out, tore the foil wrapper slowly, and rolled the condom down my length. My every thought focused on what we were about to do.

Charlie smiled when I put a little bit of lube onto the condom. "You're learning," he said, obviously pleased.

"Good teacher," I mumbled, wanting to distract myself from the erotic haze I found myself enveloped in.

"Kneel between my legs," he said, pulling them up.

After I'd positioned myself where he wanted me, he smiled. "Okay, here's the deal. You're quite a bit thicker than three fingers, and it's been a long time, so I'd appreciate it if you go slow so I have time to adjust to having you in me. Okay?"

I did my best to focus on my target. My cock throbbed so hard I feared it would burst. After scooting forward a little, I took my shaft in my hand and positioned it at his opening. "Are you sure?" I asked.

"Very" came the reply. "I've been wanting this for a year, but if you need more time, then we'll take it."

"No, I'm okay," I promised, though every nerve in my body was set to high. I put my hands on his legs as I pushed in, just a little. I made sure to keep checking his expression, needing to ensure I wasn't hurting him. As soon as the head of my cock breached his hole, this incredible pressure surrounded it. I immediately stopped, because the sensations were damned overwhelming. My teeth sank into my lower lip, the small bite of pain giving me something to think about.

"Matt? Are you okay?" Charlie asked.

155

I nodded. I could feel warmth trailing down my cheeks. I knew I was crying yet again.

"You can push in some more."

I shook my head, unable to move.

"Baby, what's wrong?" he asked me, rubbing my arms.

"I'm going to come," I said, embarrassed that it would be over any moment. "I can't make it good for you."

He gave me a warm smile. "Come if you want. You've already made it better for me. To know that I'm your first and, just so you know, your only? That's pretty goddamn heady. If you come now, then we try again later. There's nothing to be embarrassed or ashamed of."

Without replying, I pushed in a little deeper. Charlie groaned, his head thrown back and mouth open. I couldn't believe the heat that flowed around me. I had to bury myself all the way. It became my focal point. Slowly I pressed in a little deeper, each inch burning me up from the heat in his body. When I found myself unable to move any more, I realized I was fully seated inside Charlie. He squeezed his ass muscles, and I groaned at the combination of heat and tightness.

"So good," he purred. "Do you think you might be able to move now? Just pull out a little, then push back in. Find a rhythm that's comfortable for you."

Drawing in a deep breath, I slid out an inch, then bucked my hips to reseat myself.

"Yes, just like that," Charlie urged. "Do it again."

I repeated the process a few times, each movement bringing me indescribable emotions of love and admiration for the man who was giving himself to me. Judging from the sounds Charlie was making, he was enjoying it too.

"Okay now, if you want it to be really good, try going harder. Do the same thing you've been doing, but push in faster. I swear you won't hurt me, and I think you'll find it heightens the pleasure for both of us."

It could be better? Somehow I doubted that. But Charlie knew, and I trusted him. I withdrew a few inches, then shoved back in. Small quakes shuddered through my body at the realization of how absolutely amazing it felt.

"Did you like that?" he asked, giving me a cheeky grin.

Instead of answering, I did it again. And again. Over and over, I thrust into him, each time getting closer to climax. This time there would be no way I could hold back, and I didn't want to. This would be my first orgasm through actual sex! Charlie must have known how close I was, because he wrapped a hand around his own swollen cock and began to jack it. It was such an erotic sight, watching him pull in time to my thrusts.

"Getting close, Matt," he whispered. "When I come, you're going to shoot off like a rocket."

I already knew I would. Even when I was a horny teen, I'd never felt this delicious ache in my balls.

And then Charlie was orgasming onto his stomach and chest, and the most amazing thing happened. As tight as I thought he'd been before, he bore down, locking me inside of him. I might have screamed as I came, I wasn't sure, but I'd never felt anything like it. And all the while, Charlie was stroking my arms, my chest, telling me how much he loved me.

When it finally subsided, my arms and legs felt like they were made of gelatin. Charlie braced me, then lowered me onto the bed, stripped off the condom, and put it into the garbage can. Then he reached over for the towel again and wiped us down. After, he pulled me into his arms, and I was surrounded by his scent.

"That was amazing," he whispered to me. "You sure you've never done that before?" My halfhearted swat to his arm had him grinning. "You can do that to me anytime," he promised.

"What if I can't let you...?" My voice vanished. It wasn't the sweet, romantic conversation I'd expected, but I had to know.

"Oh, you're so damned amazing. I don't know what I did to deserve you." He stroked my cheek. "I told you, I love bottoming." He grinned. "And you were very, *very* good at topping."

But part of the problem was his ex had never let him top. He'd said so himself. What happened when he decided he wanted the same thing with me?

"Hey," he said, holding my chin. "Are you thinking about Mitch?"

There wasn't any way I'd lie to him, so I nodded.

"Sweetheart, listen to me very carefully. Mitch was a selfish lover. He didn't care if I got off, only if he did. You worried about making it good for me, and you did. I loved what we did, and I want to do it again. A lot. If you think you want to try it the other way, we'll do the same thing we did today. We'll take it very slow, and I'll walk you through it step-by-step. I would never do anything you were uncomfortable with."

And I knew it to be the truth. Just as I knew one day I would bottom for him. It might take some time, and I might have to talk to Dr. Rob about it, but I knew deep down, it would definitely happen.

"I love you," I said, trying to convey what my heart felt.

"And I'm always going to love you," he replied. "By the way, are you good and relaxed now?"

Oh God. I was boneless. I felt like a rag doll. "Yeah, I don't think I can move."

"Glad to hear it. So you know, I arranged it with Clay to have our wedding on Christmas Day."

I reared back. "But that's only two weeks away!"

"I know, but I figured if we didn't, you'd fret about it."

Damn. He knew me way too well.

CHAPTER NINETEEN

CHARLIE WAS still asleep when Clay called early the next morning. Apparently Charlie had been busy while he was in New York, enlisting the aid of my family to get our wedding ready. I wasn't allowed to know the details because, as Charlie said, I would fuss over every one of them. Clay was to give me my itinerary and make sure I got to every place I was supposed to go.

"Noon on Christmas Day," he said. "Before that, we'll get you a new suit, go through the guest list, and have the bachelor party."

My hands were jittery as I thought about the fact that in two weeks, I would be getting married.

"Am I making a mistake?" I asked, needing reassurance.

Clay laughed. "If you have to ask...."

"No," I admitted. "I'm sure of how I feel about Charlie. Did he tell you how he proposed?"

Clay huffed. "When I told Trish, she squeed like a little kid. Charlie really raised the bar. I don't know how I'm going to top that."

That piqued my interest. "Oh? Are you planning on asking Trish to marry you?"

Clay coughed. "Don't tell her, okay? Charlie gave me two tickets to a Broadway play that she's been raving about. *Hamilton*, I think she said it was. How he got them, I don't know. He said it was probably best if I didn't ask. I want to take her there on New Year's Day and spend a week. He had his assistant set it up for me. If you think you're nervous, imagine how I feel."

"You'll do great," I promised. "She's an amazing person. And she's getting one of the finest men I know."

Clay sniffled. "I owe Charlie so much. Not just for what he did for me, but what he's done for you. For us. After all this time, I never thought I'd have a chance to have you back in my life."

I started to say something, but Clay cut me off.

159

"And I mean, however you are. If you and Charlie want to just stay out at the cabin and continue on the way you have been, I'm for that. At least as long as you'll allow us to visit you. It doesn't matter how we do it, I just want to be part of your life again."

A heavy weight settled on my chest. Guilt over what had happened was one of the things Dr. Rob and I were working on. He assured me what I was feeling was perfectly normal and I shouldn't allow it to control me. He reminded me I'd handled the situation as best I could, given the circumstances. When I tried to protest that if I had stayed in therapy I might be better by now, he cut me off and reminded me every journey is unique. He said I couldn't judge myself against anyone else. If it had been Clay who was assaulted instead of me, there was no way to determine how he'd react. I tried hard to keep that lesson in mind.

"I might need time to myself on occasion," I told him. "Things are a lot better than they were, but there isn't really a cure. I can only learn how to cope as best as I can. But yes, I'd really like to see you and Mom as often as possible. Trish too. Especially if she's going to be my sister-in-law."

"Thank you, Matt. I'm glad to know you like her."

"Nah, I love her. She's got you wrapped around her little finger. I like watching her make you squirm."

"Wow. All these years, and you're still an ass," he teased. "God, I've missed you so much."

It gave me a warm feeling to talk with Clay like this.

"So what's up first on the agenda? Suit fitting?"

"Yup. We're driving to Bangor and spending the day there. Maybe we can stop for lunch, if you feel up to it."

I liked the plan.

"I do have a favor to ask of you, though."

"Uh-oh, here it comes."

"Seriously. What would you say about you and Charlie spending Christmas Eve and morning with me and Mom at her house? We'll decorate the tree together, just like we did when we were kids. Maybe share some old memories, and make a few new ones along the way."

I didn't even have to think about that. "It sounds like a great idea."

Charlie strode into the room and came over to where I sat. He rubbed his hand along the back of my neck, grabbed my mug, then headed for the coffeepot.

"My fiancé is awake. When do you want to head to Bangor?"

"I'm off tomorrow, if you have the time."

"I do. Pick me up around seven?"

Charlie came back and set a mug on the table, then sat next to me, as he sipped from his own. He put his hand on my knee and gave a squeeze. I might have squeaked a little, because Clay coughed.

"Yeah, okay. See you tomorrow," he said hurriedly.

We hung up, and I turned to Charlie. "So what all do I have to worry about for this wedding?"

He sipped his coffee and seemed completely content as he cuddled up next to me. "Not one thing. Clay is going to take you to get your suit, and everything else has been handled. All you need to do is show up to the courthouse on time. Clay said he made a special arrangement for us to get married that day, and I doubt he's going to want anything to go wrong."

"I think Clay has it planned down to the minute." I bit my lip before I said the next part. I had no idea if he'd be amenable to spending the holiday with my family. "I might have said we would spend the night at Mom's house for Christmas Eve, then head out from there the next day. That's okay, I hope."

He put down his coffee mug, turned, and looked me in the eye. "Why would you think it's not? I love your family, and I want to be part of it. Besides, I might be able to talk your mom into pulling out some baby pictures. I'd love to see what little Matt and Clay looked like."

"I love you. Thank you for being you."

He picked up his cup and took a sip. "I don't know how to be anyone else."

Smug bastard.

AFTER WE finished shopping, where I got a dark blue suit with gray stripes throughout, Clay took me back to Mom's house so we could

161

talk to her about Christmas. She must have been looking out the window, because as soon as I opened the door, she came flying out of the house.

"Matt," she cried, rushing down the sidewalk toward me, her arms open wide.

I stopped and waited for her, and when she reached me, I squeezed her as tight as I could. I knew she'd been baking, because I could smell the spices she'd been using and see the splotches of flour that dotted her shirt. I didn't care. It was a sign I was home. As for the hug? I needed my mom more than I'd ever thought I could.

"Come in," she said, taking me by the hand.

I looked at her as we walked and noticed things I hadn't when we were together the last time. She'd gotten much older. Her hair, which had been a chestnut brown, now was mostly gray. Her laugh lines formed crow's feet at the corners of her eyes. And she was thinner than I remembered. But her smile was just as bright. And her love for Clay and me was obvious in the way she fussed over us, urging us to take a seat while she went and got us something to drink.

As we sat down with a plate of gingerbread cookies and a hot drink—I declined the coffee and had some hot apple cider instead—Clay told her about his idea for us to come together for the holiday. Suffice it to say, she was thrilled with the idea. She had us go into the attic and haul down all the boxes with the supplies that had been stored up there for so many years. I lost count of the number of things we carried, but with each box, Mom's excitement grew.

"This is going to be wonderful," she declared. "Any thoughts about what you'd like for Christmas dinner?"

Every year for Christmas, we would have chicken and stuffing, cranberry sauce that Mom made, and whipped potatoes with gravy. The house would smell absolutely amazing for the entire day as she stood in the kitchen and sliced, diced, sautéed, boiled. God, even now, I can remember waking up to those amazing scents.

"What about what we always had?" I asked, then looked at Clay. "Would that work for you?"

He grinned. "I was hoping you'd say that."

OVER THE remainder of the week, Charlie had me bouncing around with Clay and Mom, looking at things to decorate the house with, gifts we wanted to give my family, and the like. He claimed he needed time to discuss a book tour with his publisher. He said he'd asked not to go on this one, as he was getting married. Allegedly they raised a fuss about it, so he was talking to them. Curiouser and curiouser.

Christmas Eve we arrived at my mother's house at four in the afternoon. She had the tree set up in the living room, just like we used to do. You can't imagine how much fun we all had decorating the thing. The tree was beautiful. Six feet tall, it stood proud as the centerpiece of the room. We had decorated it with almost a thousand twinkling lights and kitschy little baubles, but when Mom pulled out the box marked "precious," my heart stopped. Bulbs that held pictures of her and my dad were hung on slender strings. Ornaments that Clay and I had made in school were there, ready to be placed on the tree. Every one of them brought memories. When she pulled out the star and handed it to me, I had to fight back the tears. There was no way it was the original. That got ruined when the tree got knocked over as Clay and I fought about some stupid gift. But it looked exactly like.... *Shit.*

"Mom?"

"Yes?"

"Is this the actual star?"

She smiled at me and took it from my hands, gazing fondly at it for a moment. Then she showed me where a few chips were missing, but also where other parts were put back together with glue or something. "I saved it," she said, running her fingers over it. "It took a few tries before I realized it wasn't unlike putting a puzzle together." She twirled it. The light refracted and made tiny colored spinning dots on all of us. "I guess I could have thrown it away, but your father picked it out when you were born, and I couldn't get rid of it. Guess I'm just sentimental that way."

Emotions overwhelmed me. Memories of my father, the hugs on Christmas morning that ended when he died. Our first Christmas after that was somber, and it dawned on me that's what it was probably like for Clay and Mom after I left. I stumbled back a half step, and Charlie was there right away. He wrapped his arms around my shoulders. When Mom handed the star back to me, I offered it to my brother, but he shook his head.

"Go ahead and put it up. This is the start of a new year for us, so it's only fitting that you do it."

My hands trembled when I got up and walked to the tree. I was deathly afraid the star would fall and shatter again. It had to be perfect, because in my mind, it symbolized me coming home once again.

"Charlie?" I whispered, unable to move. "Help me."

Immediately he was by my side. He held my hands to steady them and helped me put the ornament at the top of the tree.

"It's beautiful," he whispered to me, right before he buried his face in my neck, kissing me gently.

"It looks perfect," Clay said.

Charlie pulled me back to the couch, and the four of us sat quietly, each lost in our own thoughts and memories.

Afterward, Mom served dinner. My stomach was still knotted, and I didn't eat as much as I could have, but the food was delicious. When we'd finished the meal, we retired to the living room again, to bask in the presence of the tree. Mom, Clay, and I sat up until nearly midnight, catching up. When I asked Charlie to join us, he begged off, saying I needed the time to reconnect with my family, but if I needed him, he'd always be there for me.

I sat and listened intently as Mom told me about going back to work part time as a crossing guard for the local elementary school. She only put in fifteen hours a week, but she loved having the chance to be around kids. I nudged Clay and told him he'd better get on the ball if he was going to give Mom a grandchild to spoil. He turned it back on me and said that more and more gay men were having families, and Charlie and I should consider it for ourselves. I quickly changed the subject, but the thought was planted in my head. Maybe it would be something to talk to Charlie about at some point.

Sitting around the kitchen table, the same one Mom had when I still lived at home, was strange. It seemed as though almost no time had passed, but the reality of the situation was still evident. We kept the conversation light, none of us seeming to want to disrupt the tentative bond we were rebuilding. That was okay with me. I was content just sitting there and simply being Matt.

As we talked, the conversation turned to Christmases I'd missed. There wasn't any censure on their parts, but there was a prevailing sadness that the three of us shared. When I tried, yet again, to apologize, they both stopped me and said they wanted to look to the future and hopes of many more holidays together. I knew they were trying to be nice, and I accepted the wish.

Mom went to bed a little after midnight, reminding me that someone—not mentioning any names—would be awake early to open gifts. Clay sputtered and said he'd outgrown that phase long ago. She gave me a knowing wink, then went on to bed.

Clay got up and made us each a cup of cocoa. He stirred in some marshmallows, a treat from when we were kids, and then we went back into the living room and sat staring at the tree. I counted the seconds until Clay couldn't stand it anymore.

He picked up a box and gave it a shake. "It's going to be clothes," he complained. "I miss the model race cars and things like that. Remember that year she gave us each a radio-controlled plane?"

I laughed at the memory, because it had resulted in the two of us going out to play with them. We'd argued over which was fastest, who could fly higher, and then which one would come out on top if we intentionally crashed into one another. Suffice it to say, neither did. Each of us pointed at the other as bits of plastic and metal rained down, trying to shift the blame, when we both knew we had both been at fault. Mom just shook her head over the whole mess and made us clean it up.

I finished my drink, washed out my cup, and put it back with the others. As soon as I closed the cabinet door, strong arms encircled my waist.

"The bed is lonely," Charlie complained.

I turned and received a kiss. When I tried to say something, Charlie pointed above the door at the mistletoe. "I'm not standing under it," I said.

"Preemptive kiss," he claimed, then took another.

"You two look good together," Clay said, entering the kitchen to put his cup into the dishwasher. He gave us a wistful smile. "Though it does make me wish Trish was here."

"She's coming in the morning, right?"

Trish worked overnight for the Gianettis, stocking shelves and doing general cleaning. It was where she and Clay met, in fact, when he stopped in one night, desperate for a coffee fix. It wasn't much as far as a job went, but they paid her well, and she said they treated her like she was valuable, and she appreciated that.

"She should be here by five. Mr. Gianetti told her she could have the night off, but she said there wasn't anyone else to work. She can't wait. She's never been to a big old gay wedding before. I told her the two of you would be dressed up in lavender tuxes, with enormous pink boutonnières. I don't know if she thinks I'm serious or not, but the look on her face was well worth it."

Charlie shook his head. "I'm so glad I'm going to be a member of this family," he stated. "You all are awesome."

A quick shrug of his shoulder, a grin, and Clay announced he was going to retire for the night.

I nudged Charlie. "He's going to be up at four, trying to get the rest of us to wake up and open gifts."

"You know I outgrew that, right?" Clay said again, but not too convincingly.

His indignation made me laugh. I had missed Clay during the holidays. He had a warm, giving spirit. Mom had told me the sheriff's office ran a Toys for Tots drive every year, and Clay spent hundreds of dollars to ensure that every kid in the area who needed a happy holiday would find something under the tree with their name on it. As proud as I was that Clay was the sheriff, the fact that he grew up to be a decent human being was even better.

CHAPTER TWENTY

"NERVOUS?" CLAY asked as he straightened my bow tie.

"How can you tell?" I shot back, then ducked my head. "Sorry."

He reached out and rubbed my shoulder. "There isn't anything to worry about. Charlie loves you," Clay reminded me. "Hell, seeing the two of you together, I might even be a little jealous. Trish doesn't look at me like that. What's your secret?"

"It's the whole gay thing, of course."

He gave me a smirk. "Do you think if I switch to men, you'll get credit for it?"

"I might! And I'm so close to earning that toaster, that would go a long way." I laughed at his expression before Clay wrapped me in a hug.

"Thank you for asking me to be here with you."

It was going to be a small ceremony, only family and the judge. I was so hyped by what lay ahead, my pills barely took the edge off. Mom was here, as was Clay—who was going to act as my best man, even though it was a civil ceremony, and he'd brought Trish with him. Charlie's sister had come to stand with him, and she had been crying buckets before we'd even gotten inside the courthouse. Charlie's parents had flown in, and when I first met them, his mother hugged me and his father nearly broke my spine. I loved them right away.

I'd invited Dr. Rob, but he'd declined. I wasn't upset about it, but I would have felt weird if I hadn't at least let him know he was welcome. Mr. Gianetti and his wife had come. He was surprised when I asked, but he had kept me well-stocked with groceries for years. Plus, I got to meet his family. It was fun watching Mrs. Gianetti fuss over her husband, and despite his complaints, I knew he loved her.

"I'm glad you said yes," I told Clay. "Having you here makes me a little calmer."

"It's not too late for us to jump in the car and head for Canada," Clay reminded me. "We could become lumberjacks or Hungry Jacks or something."

That made me chuckle. "For the first time in my life, I feel like I belong somewhere. Charlie's incredible, and having him up at the house with me has made it into a home. And having him here makes me feel… I'm not even sure how to express it."

"Maybe complete? I know the pills help, but you seemed much calmer around him even before you started taking them."

I thought back. "Yeah, complete is a good word. My touchstones used to be my books and things. But now, if I need reassurance, the first thing I do is look for Charlie. He's always able to ground me with a touch."

A knock on the door had me drawing in a deep breath. The moment I'd been waiting for—and fearing—had finally arrived.

"Showtime," I said, my hands a little shaky.

"It's fine. Just us. Remember that. Everyone in that room is your family."

We stepped into the hall. There wasn't anyone around since it was the holiday, which made things a little easier. As we entered the room, I saw everyone turn toward Clay and me. They all smiled, and Mr. Gianetti gave a small wave, which turned into him wiping his eyes. Then my gaze was drawn to where Charlie stood. He'd chosen a charcoal gray suit and burgundy tie. He looked so handsome standing there, waiting for me. He grinned when he saw me, and I felt my body heat.

At the front of the room stood the last man I'd ever expected to be presiding over a marriage between two men. Judge Hamlin had always seemed to be a bitter, homophobic old man when I had him as a teacher, but when he saw me, his eyes twinkled.

"Matthew, it's very good to see you out and about," he said. "I'm honored I was asked to officiate this wedding."

Clay urged me forward. When I stood next to Charlie, he reached for my hand.

"I know this is a civil ceremony, but if the two gentlemen don't mind, I have something I'd like to say," Judge Hamlin said.

Charlie's brow furrowed, and his grip tightened slightly. "Okay."

"Thank you." Judge Hamlin turned his attention to the sparse number of people with us and cleared his throat. "I've known Matt since he was my student in high school. I could stand up here and wax lyrical about what an amazing person he was, but I won't do that. Each and every one of you knows exactly what kind of person he is. When he withdrew from the community, we were the ones who lost out. His capacity for giving was one of his best features. He always stood up for others. Never had I seen him talk down to anyone, with maybe the exception of his younger brother."

Everyone laughed, and Clay got up and waved, which made them roar.

Judge Hamlin stood there and waited for the people to calm down before he continued. "Matt constantly reminded me of why I became a teacher. Yes, I rode him harder than anyone else, because there was so much potential in him. And then, in a moment, someone he'd trusted, someone he'd tried to help, snuffed it out."

I tried to draw away from Charlie, but he held fast, his eyes locked on the officiant. I could see the anger in his gaze, and feared he was about to say something, but Judge Hamlin spoke again.

"At least I thought they'd snuffed it out. You see, Matt proved himself to be a strong individual in the most trying of times. He pulled himself up, dusted himself off, and forged a life. It's not one most of us would choose for ourselves, because it wasn't an easy one. He had only himself to rely on. However, if there is one thing I can say with absolute certainty, it's that if you ever needed a person to put your faith in, Matt would be the one."

Warmth flooded my body. Choices I wished I had made no longer seemed relevant. Today was the only thing I needed to think about.

"And now," Judge Hamlin continued, "he stands here with another man who is a recent addition to our community. Someone who helped Matt blossom once again. And they've asked me to be a part of the melding of their lives. I can honestly say, never in my years as a teacher, as a lawyer, or as a judge, have I ever been so proud to be here while a member of our family comes home again."

Charlie wrapped me in his arms and whispered, "Wow. I'm marrying a celebrity." When he stepped back, he turned to Judge Hamlin. "Thank you for what you said. It's great to know that people think so highly of Matt."

Judge Hamlin's voice cracked a bit when he said, "I wanted to be there for him, but respected his wishes to be left alone. In hindsight, it was a failure on my part. I'm sorry for that, Matt."

"Thank you," I replied.

"Okay, I think these two men have waited long enough to be married! So, are you both ready? Who has the rings?"

"I do," Clay replied.

"Great. I'd say join hands, but I see that's already accomplished," Judge Hamlin said, nodding toward us. "Matt, today in front of those gathered here, you're adding another branch to your family tree. When we graft one onto the other, it takes a lot of love, careful tending, and faith for it to grow strong enough to help support the whole. Do you think the man who stands beside you possesses the maturity, wisdom, and stamina to help your tree grow?"

"Yes. I do."

Judge Hamlin winked at me. "I thought you might." He turned his attention to Charlie. "Charles Carver, you're here today to accept this branch for your own tree. It's been tested and proven its strength, but it's also a bit frail. Do you have the internal fortitude to help it flourish and once again blossom like it should have all those years ago? Yours is the toughest job, because this branch will depend on you in ways you might not have discovered yet. Do you think the man beside you possesses the character, the intellect, and the love to help your tree grow?"

"I do."

"Then by the power vested in me by the great state of Maine, I happily pronounce your trees grafted."

"Still on the horticulture kick?" Clay teased.

"Hey, it works for trees and for people," I replied.

"Okay, now the two of you can go ahead and kiss. And make it a good one, because there will be pictures you're going to have to see for the rest of your lives."

Charlie pulled me toward him and wrapped a hand around my neck. He held me close, whispered he loved me, then brought our mouths together. While I heard the clicking of cell phones and cameras, nothing distracted me from pouring every bit of love I possessed for this man into my kiss. When we parted, we were surrounded by our family, who'd come to congratulate us. I was delighted they'd been here to share this moment.

Nothing could be more perfect than this place, this time. For so many years I hid away, afraid of the world. Charlie, who now had his arm wrapped around my waist, had brought me back to life again. He'd shown me that some things are worth fighting for.

He'd shown me I was.

"We have a reception at the hall across the street," Mr. Gianetti told me. "The boys are over there setting it up, and when you're ready, we'll go on over and eat."

"You're not getting cheesecake," Mrs. Gianetti admonished. "There are some perfectly good berries on the buffet. Eat as much of that as you want."

He glared at her, then grinned when she pinched his cheeks.

"I love you, you know."

The way he smiled, I could tell he did.

We went to the hall Clay had rented. Mr. Gianetti's sons, all four of them, had just finished setting everything up. There were bowls of shrimp on ice, serving dishes with fried chicken, pork chops, breaded mushrooms and cheese sticks, onion rings, rows of pastries, ice cream, and the most beautiful cake I'd ever seen, with two miniature grooms atop it.

"Wow," I said, which I knew was the understatement of the year. "This is amazing."

Mrs. Gianetti came over and pulled me against her. "Theo thinks of you like one of his own, you know. If one of the boys was to get married—and God, please let it be soon—this would be his gift to them too."

"But this is a lot of food for so few people."

She shrugged and let go of me. "Theo believes food is a great equalizer. From kings to paupers, everyone eats, he says. So one person or one hundred, he's going to make sure you never forget this night."

As she said that, Mr. Gianetti strode over and kissed her on the cheek. He had a thick slice of cheesecake in his hand. She frowned at him, but when he gave her a smile, she melted.

"One piece," she said, wagging a finger at him.

"Yes, dear. Of course. I would never have more than one."

She turned to me. "He thinks I didn't see the other one he ate when he was at the dessert table."

He scowled at her, then smiled and kissed her on the cheek. I laughed, because even I could see the amount of love between them.

"You've got a great family," Mr. Gianetti said as he and his wife walked away. "You ought to be proud."

And I was.

When I glanced at my watch, I was surprised—but happy—to see how much time had passed. It was already after six, and I had been able to keep myself calm by focusing on other things. Like watching my family and Charlie's mingle. His mother had mine in one corner of the room. They both had their phones out and were making *aww* faces, so I guessed they were sharing pictures. Charlie had danced with everyone at least once—including Clay, at Trish's urging—and they'd been laughing when they left the dance floor, hand in hand. Clay had even given Charlie a hug before he grabbed Trish up in his arms and carried her out so they could share a dance.

As I watched them, seeing the love that was almost palpable between them, Teresa swooped in. "Congratulations. You've got yourself a good man."

"Don't I know it," I told her, watching as Mrs. Gianetti loaded up a plate for Charlie, whose eyes went wide at the amount of food she was giving him.

"I have to tell you, I have never seen this side of Charlie before. I thought he and Mitch were in love, but seeing him with you? That dreamy expression he gets whenever he looks at you?" She shrugged. "He never once had that with Mitch. But Charlie is ever the gentleman. I didn't know that Mitch had cheated on him. Charlie said they agreed to some mutual time away. I just assumed they'd get back together. This Charlie? The one you married today? He's a way better man."

"Thank you," I said, my throat a little dry. "He makes me better too."

"You'll be good to him, right?" she asked, then bit her lip.

"Of course. I—"

Her parents came walking up to us. "Ignore Teresa. She likes to think of Charlie as *her* baby. Welcome to the family, Matt," Gail said, giving me another hug.

The whole lot of them seemed to be huggers, and it was something I would need to get used to.

"The ceremony was beautiful. I like the judge."

"Yeah, I thought he hated me when I was a kid. Live and learn, I guess."

"You look like a man who could use some saving," Charlie said as he strode over to us. He held out his hand. "Can I have this dance?"

"If you don't mind risking broken toes, yes."

He led me out onto the dance floor and took me in his arms. "This night? It's pure magic," he said. "I've pinched myself at least a dozen times to prove I'm not dreaming."

I wouldn't tell him I'd done the same.

As the evening wore down, Charlie and I went out, enjoying the nip in the air. The sky was a tapestry of stars against a black backdrop. The moon hung pendulously overhead, so big and bright you would think you could actually reach out and pluck it from the sky.

"Well, Mr. Bowers, how do you think it went?"

I turned and gazed into his eyes. "I think the phrase you used said it best. Pure magic. A year ago, if you had said I would be standing up in front of a group of people, saying I would gladly take someone's hand in marriage, I would have scoffed and then said you were wrong. Now? I swear I can't remember a time when you weren't a part of my life. It's like everything else is the dream, and now reality starts from here."

He bent down and kissed me again. That light-headed, dizzy feeling I got when he did? I hoped never to lose it.

"You know, if I hadn't gotten home that night, I would have married Mitch. I would have played at being happy, but I wouldn't have been. And knowing he was cheating while we were together?

Makes me wonder if he would have stopped if we had gone ahead with a wedding."

"I don't know the answer to that. But his loss? It's my gain."

"You always know the nicest things to say," he said, kissing my neck.

"Well, when you have a writer in the family, you tend to pick up a few things."

He laughed, and his breath fogged the air.

"I'm getting cold," I told him. "Can we go home so you can warm me up?"

"I think that's the best idea I've heard today."

We walked back to where Charlie had parked at City Hall. I didn't want to catch a ride with anyone else. The night was simply too perfect to let it go by. He held my hand the whole way home, being attentive and sweet. It felt wrong of me, but I was glad his ex was a lying cheat, because he'd given me a gift. I briefly wondered if it would be in poor form to send a thank-you card. I decided it probably would be, but the idea still made me smile a little.

He drove us back to the house, and when we got inside, he pinned me against the door and kissed me as he undressed me. An owl hooted from one of the trees, and the wind had picked up a little, but the night couldn't be better.

"I need you tonight, Matt. I want to fall asleep in your arms. I want the first day of our new life to be special."

"Sounds good to me!"

"No, you don't understand. I *need* you. Every bit of you has to surround me, and make me yours. Show me what it's like to be married to the man I love."

I hesitated, and he must have known what was in my mind.

"I don't mean sex. I mean intimacy. I just want you to touch me. Please?"

"That sounds good," I said, taking him into the bedroom and watching as he began to strip off his clothes. Though they were our good things, we threw them haphazardly about the room. Decorum

174

had gone out the window, and it had been replaced by a deep, gnawing need to simply be together.

That night as we lay in bed, we whispered words of love. We touched each other tenderly, asking for nothing more than being with each other. It was, in my mind, the most perfect night I'd ever had, but I wondered if it could last.

I pulled my lips from Charlie's. "Ask you a question?"

"Of course," he panted.

"Are you really okay with living here? I mean, you said New York was a better place for a writer. We could—"

Charlie laughed and squeezed my hand. "No, we can't. I told you before, and will tell you as often as needed, this house, this land? It's my home. Nothing has ever been more perfect than being here with you. I would give up writing before I give up this life."

"But what about Donald and Lucien? Don't they have more to say?"

He turned to me and propped his head up on his hand. "Well, you finished the book. You tell me."

It had been a roller-coaster ride until the end. In a last-minute blaze of glory, Donald had proven Lucien's innocence, captured the real killer via an elaborate plan to gain his confession, and then, to top it off, he'd gotten married to the man he loved. Then the two of them boarded a cruise ship for their honeymoon, leaving for parts unknown.

"I did. I think it was the best book in the series. But is that how the story ends?"

Charlie snuggled up against me. "What do you think?"

Through all their hardships and the pain, the two of them had forged a life together. They were made stronger by the love they shared. They were yin and yang. Two parts that needed to come together to be whole. Afterward, they got together and sailed off into an apparent ending to the series, the thought of which saddened me.

"I don't think it is," I admitted. "A story like that doesn't get to end. It goes on and on."

"You mean like ours?" he whispered, his voice full of sleep.

"What? What does that mean?"

He yawned and put his head back down on his pillow. "A lot of folks will look at this as our happily ever after, but it's not. What we have here, right now? It's only the beginning of our story. The rest is yet to be written."

And with those words and a soft smile, Charlie drifted off to sleep. I followed behind shortly after.

PARKER WILLIAMS began to write as a teen, but never showed his work to anyone. As he grew older, he drifted away from writing, but his love of the written word moved him to reading. A chance encounter with an author changed the course of his life as she encouraged him to never give up on a dream. With the help of some amazing friends, he rediscovered the joy of writing, thanks to a community of writers who have become his family.

Parker firmly believes in love, but is also of the opinion that anything worth having requires work and sacrifice (plus a little hurt and angst, too). The course of love is never a smooth one, and happily-ever-after always has a price tag.

Website: www.parkerwilliamsauthor.com
Twitter: @ParkerWAuthor
Facebook: www.facebook.com/parker.williams.75641
Email: parker@parkerwilliamsauthor.com

BEFORE
YOU
BREAK
SECRETS

K.C. WELLS & PARKER WILLIAMS

Six years ago Ellis walked into his first briefing as the newest member of London's Specialist Firearms unit. He was partnered with Wayne and they became fast friends. When Wayne begins to notice changes—Ellis's erratic temper, the effects of sleep deprivation—he knows he has to act before Ellis reaches his breaking point. He invites Ellis to the opening of the new BDSM club, Secrets, where Wayne has a membership. His purpose? He wants Ellis to glimpse the lifestyle before Wayne approaches him with a proposition. He wants to take Ellis in hand, to control his life because he wants his friend back, and he figures this is the only way to do it.

There are a few issues, however. Ellis is straight. Stubborn. And sexy. Wayne knows he has to put his own feelings aside to be what Ellis needs. What surprises the hell out of him is finding out what Ellis actually requires.

www.dreamspinnerpress.com

COLLARS & CUFFS NOVEL

SOMEONE TO
KEEP ME

K.C. WELLS & PARKER WILLIAMS

Collars and Cuffs: Book Three

Eighteen-year-old Scott Keating knows a whole world exists beyond his parents' strict control, but until he gains access to the World Wide Web, he really has no idea what's out there. In a chat room, Scott meets "JeffUK." Jeff loves and understands him, and when he offers to bring Scott to the UK, Scott seizes his chance to escape his humdrum life and see the world. But when his plane touches down and Jeff isn't there, panic sets in.

Collars & Cuffs favorite barman and Dom-in-training, Ben Winters, drops his sister off at the airport and finds a lost, anxious Scott. Hearing Scott's story sets off alarm bells, along with his protective instincts. Taking pity on the naïve boy, Ben offers him a place to crash and invites him to Collars & Cuffs, hoping his bosses will know how to help. Scott dreams of belonging to someone, heart and soul. Ben longs for a sub of his own. And neither man sees what's right under his nose.

www.dreamspinnerpress.com

COLLARS & CUFFS

DAMIAN'S DISCIPLINE

K.C. WELLS & PARKER WILLIAMS

Collars and Cuffs: Book Five

The man who pimped Jeff may be in prison, but Jeff is still living the nightmare, selling himself to men and relying on pills to manage. Then he meets Scott, a young American man who could easily have been where Jeff is now. Scott's friends extend a helping hand to Jeff, and he grabs it.

Leo and Thomas bring Jeff to stay with Dom Damian Barnett until they can find him someplace more long-term. Still grieving from losing his sub to cancer two years before, Damian agrees to help. But when he glimpses the extent of the damage, Damian wants to do more than offer his guestroom. Jeff is not a submissive, but Damian can see he desperately needs structure in his life. It's up to Damian to find an answer.

He never expects that what he discovers will change both their lives.

www.dreamspinnerpress.com

COLLARS & CUFFS

DOM OF
AGES

K.C. WELLS & PARKER WILLIAMS

Collars and Cuffs: Book Seven

Eli may only be thirty, but he has had enough of pretend submissives. When he spies Jarod in a BDSM club, everything about the man screams submission. So what if Jarod is probably twenty years older than Eli. What does age matter, anyway? All he can see is what he's always wanted—a sub who wants to serve.

Jarod spent twenty-four years with his Master before Fate took him. Four years on, Jarod is still lost, so when a young Dom takes charge, Jarod rolls with it and finds himself serving again. But he keeps waiting for the other shoe to drop. Because there's going to come a point when Eli realizes he's a laughingstock in the club. Who would want to be seen with a fifty-year-old sub?

After several missteps, Eli realizes that in order to find happiness, they will need friends who will understand. At a friend's insistence, he visits Collars & Cuffs, where they are met with open arms. As they settle in to their new life, Eli begins to see things differently and he dares to think he can have it all. Until a phone call threatens to take it all away....

www.dreamspinnerpress.com

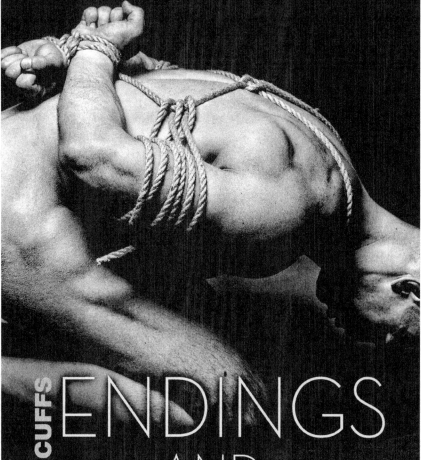

COLLARS & CUFFS

ENDINGS
AND
BEGINNINGS

K.C. WELLS & PARKER WILLIAMS

Collars and Cuffs: Book Eight

In all his relationships, Darren Fielding never found the level of intimacy he witnessed between Thomas Williams and his sub, Peter, the day of Peter's "rebirth." Not only that, he never realized such intimacy was possible. For two years, Thomas's business card has been burning a hole in his wallet. When Darren's lover moves on, maybe it's finally time to see where that card takes him.

Collars & Cuffs' new barman, JJ Taylor, is really conflicted right now. He went to the club with a very specific purpose, already convinced of what he'd find there. Except it's not what he expected at all. He certainly didn't anticipate finding himself drawn to the new wannabe Dom. Nor could he have guessed the direction that attraction would lead him.

Old love, new love, vows, pain, rage, moving in, moving on…. The members of Collars & Cuffs face an event that touches some of them deeply, but it will only reinforce what they already know: together they are stronger, and some bonds cannot be broken.

www.dreamspinnerpress.com

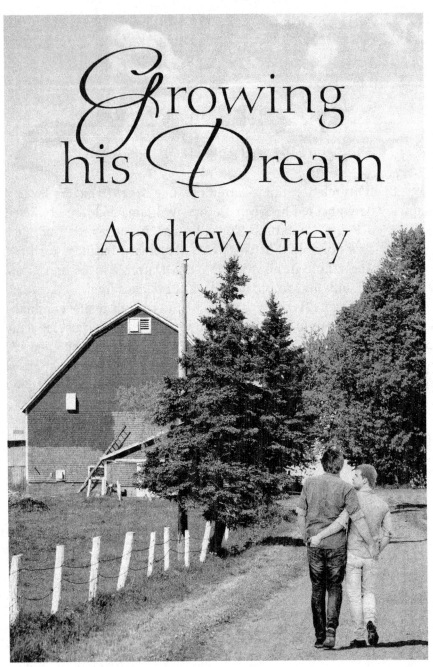

Growing his Dream

Andrew Grey

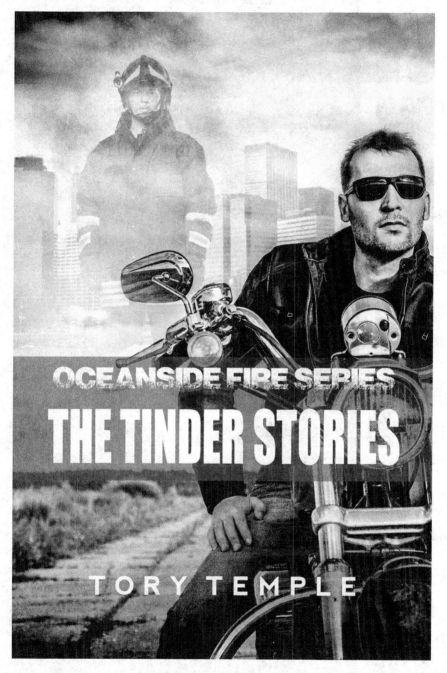

CPSIA information can be obtained
at www.ICGtesting.com
Printed in the USA
FSOW03n2334211117
41236FS